The quick _____ ng
Fargo to kee_____ck.
It was round and tapered like a walking staff, and Fargo
pulled the dark figure to him, trying to get a look at the
face under the hood. But the night was too dark and the
fog too thick.

Fargo gave a sharp twist, hoping to wrest the stick from
the figure's grasp, but the man managed to hold on. And
he quit jabbing. He simply thrust the stick into Fargo's
midsection and pushed Fargo backward with all his
strength.

Fargo felt the deck railing at his back, and then his feet
slipped as he tipped over. The figure jerked the stick away
from Fargo's fingers and jolted the Trailsman under the
chin. Fargo's teeth clicked together as he flipped over the
railing, and then he was falling, with nothing to catch him
except the muddy water of the Mississippi.

THE
TRAILSMAN
#258

CASINO
CARNAGE

by

Jon Sharpe

Ⓤ
A SIGNET BOOK

SIGNET
Published by New American Library, a division of
Penguin Putnam Inc., 375 Hudson Street,
New York, New York 10014, U.S.A.
Penguin Books Ltd, 80 Strand,
London WC2R 0RL, England
Penguin Books Australia Ltd, 250 Camberwell Road,
Camberwell, Victoria 3124, Australia
Penguin Books Canada Ltd, 10 Alcorn·Avenue,
Toronto, Ontario, Canada M4V 3B2
Penguin Books (N.Z.) Ltd, Cnr Rosedale and Airborne Roads,
Albany, Auckland 1310, New Zealand

Penguin Books Ltd, Registered Offices:
Harmondsworth, Middlesex, England

First published by Signet, an imprint of New American Library,
a division of Penguin Putnam Inc.

First Printing, April 2003
10 9 8 7 6 5 4 3 2 1

The first chapter of this book originally appeared in *Colorado Cutthroats,*
the two hundred fifty-seventh volume in this series.

 REGISTERED TRADEMARK—MARCA REGISTRADA

Printed in the United States of America

PUBLISHER'S NOTE
This is a work of fiction. Names, characters, places, and incidents either are the
product of the author's imagination or are used fictitiously, and any resemblance to
actual persons, living or dead, events, business establishments, or locales is entirely
coincidental.

The Trailsman

Beginnings . . . they bend the tree and they mark the man. Skye Fargo was born when he was eighteen. Terror was his midwife, vengeance his first cry. Killing spawned Skye Fargo, ruthless, cold-blooded murder. Out of the acrid smoke of gunpowder still hanging in the air, he rose, cried out a promise never forgotten.

The Trailsman they began to call him all across the West: searcher, scout, hunter, the man who could see where others only looked, his skills for hire but not his soul, the man who lived each day to the fullest, yet trailed each tomorrow. Skye Fargo, the Trailsman, the seeker who could take the wildness of a land and the wanting of a woman and make them his own.

Mississippi River, 1861—
After the last card has been dealt and the hand called—
sometimes the best ace in the hole
is a loaded gun.

1

Skye Fargo's lake-blue eyes narrowed. After a brief moment of contemplation he threw his five poker cards on the table in front of him. "Fold," he said. A pair of deuces wasn't going to get him much.

In spite of the bad hand, Fargo thought that a steamboat casino was an inviting place to play cards. The owner of this boat, *The Wanderer,* had invested considerable money in turning what could have been a large, crude room into a well-appointed den of parquet flooring, flocked wine-colored wallpaper with matching draperies, and enough games of chance to keep two hundred gamblers busy all at the same time.

The blackjack, faro, and squirrel-cage tables took up the east section of the casino while the west was filled with various games involving dice and four small, round tables devoted to cards. Attractive ladies employed by the casino walked among the gamblers, carrying trays of glasses filled with good whiskey and even better champagne. A gambler in his cups was an ideal gambler—he'd keep on playing even if he was losing heavily.

A man named Cameron Winthrop said, "I think Mr. Fargo is afraid to win. I think Mr. Astor here has got him scared."

There were six of them at the table. Three of them smiled. Not Fargo, nor Astor.

"If you believe those stories about me," David Astor said, "then you also believe in ghosties and goblins." He put as much sneer into his voice as he could.

"You have to admit, Astor," said Robert Daly, "it is

1

kind of strange that four of the men who won big against you were found dead within a day's time."

"Very strange," said Kenneth Shaw.

"That damned magazine article," Astor said, sounding miserable despite the smile he'd forced his mouth to imitate.

The magazine article was the reason Skye Fargo, the Trailsman, was on the boat tonight, when he'd much rather have been somewhere else, somewhere less closed in, somewhere open to the sky.

For Men Only, a rival publication of *The Police Gazette,* had published an article about a gambler named David Astor and how, over the course of a year, every man who took home a considerable pot from one of his poker tables, four thousand dollars being the smallest of these, didn't live to see much beyond the next morning's sunrise.

The magazine didn't say explicitly that Astor himself had killed the men. But the author had implied it. And while a few gamblers who practiced their craft up and down the Mississippi River generally laughed the Astor story off as a bizarre coincidence, many took it quite seriously. Even those who didn't often kidded Astor about it without mercy.

Daly and Shaw were professional gamblers and had known Astor for years. Tonight, as most nights, they joked tirelessly about him and about each other. Sometimes there was an unpleasant edge to their humor that made Fargo wonder just how genuine their friendship for Astor really was.

Cameron Winthrop was another matter. He was a fierce, stocky man with the manner of a plantation owner. He seemed to believe that every other creature who trod the planet was his natural-born slave. In his expensive, dark Eastern-made suit, he looked the rich, spoiled man he was. He'd started chiding Astor about the article early in the evening and kept it up as midnight approached and the crowd of elegant men and women began to thin.

Because of the article, Astor had stayed away from the river for three months. Now he was gambling again, which worried his younger sister, Chloe, with whom the Trailsman had spent a blissful week once upon a time. Chloe had wired Fargo and asked him to accompany David on his trip from the Minnesota border all the way down to New Orleans.

So here he sat, playing cards and studying the men around the table. Fargo had the notion that the real killer—the person killing the players who won big against Astor—was likely somebody the young man knew. Somebody who believed he had a reason to hate David and wanted to torture him. Killing David would be too easy; he'd rather make him suffer by killing off the players who won his money. Make him such a pariah that people would be afraid to play with him. Then, maybe someday, actually get around to killing him off. If the law didn't do it first. There were four sheriffs up and down the big river who believed that Astor had killed the men, and if they could get any proof at all, Astor's days were numbered.

The man winning big tonight—the sixth man at the table—was a tipsy Colorado businessman named Fred Hollister, a novice poker player. Watching him try to cut the deck was almost embarrassing, like watching a bad vaudeville act. But the gods had blessed him this evening.

He'd already won more than thirty-five hundred dollars, and he'd done so while being distracted by the bodies and charms of the roaming casino ladies. He was a grabber and a pincher and a patter, and the other men at the table were always warning him to leave the ladies alone and get back to gambling.

And for him, the gambling was going very well. It seemed that he could do no wrong. Half the time he didn't even ask for new cards, and he got so tipsy that he started knocking things over—cards, drinks, ashtrays.

Gamblers rarely brought their wives or girlfriends along on river trips. But for businessmen like Hollister and Winthrop, wives were along on every trip, and wives tended to show up to warn husbands that it was time to retire for the evening.

Mrs. Hollister was there first. A fleshy matron with an unexpectedly sweet face and manner, she stood with her hands on her husband's shoulders, only occasionally whispering for him to go. Hollister patted his wife's hands fondly when he wasn't reaching for one of the girls who drifted by. His wife tolerated his behavior with apparent good nature.

3

Then came Mrs. Winthrop, and the very air was charged with the kind of sexual undercurrent that quickly pulled down red-blooded men of all ages. None of the players could concentrate on their cards.

At one point, Winthrop demanded, "Will you stupid bastards quit staring at my wife and play poker?"

It was clear that the man most taken with Ida Winthrop was David Astor. He lost three hands in a row and barely seemed aware of it. From what Fargo could see, the Winthrop woman was equally taken with Astor.

And so the game went for the final forty minutes—the players greatly distracted by Ida Winthrop. Hollister was finally talked into quitting by his wife after he spilled another drink, this time all over the crotch of his tan summer suit.

Cam Winthrop was drunk, too. But where Hollister was a happy drunk, Winthrop was angry and suspicious of everything.

"No you don't," he snapped at Fargo when the Trailsman cut the deck for one more hand. "You waited till I was distracted to cut them. Now cut them again in front of me."

Fargo shrugged. It wasn't worth arguing about, not with a drunk. He cut the cards again.

But Winthrop's main opponent was not Fargo; David Astor took that role. For the last six hands, Winthrop had maneuvered the game so that he and Astor were the only two still tossing money into the pot. The last game Winthrop obviously felt he'd won—a trio of jacks, queen high. But then he saw the cards Astor laid on the table.

A trio of queens, a pair of threes.

"You're trash!" Winthrop shouted imperiously. "Every goddamned one of you! River trash! Gutter trash!"

By now, most of the people in the casino were aware that a scene was playing out. In casinos, scenes happened with the regularity of busted flushes. Casino regulars were used to raised voices, shoving matches, bellowed threats. They'd pay each a minute or two of attention, then go back to their games.

Winthrop grabbed his wife and tore her away from the casino. But not before she got one last lingering look at David Astor.

Astor was still staring at the space the beautiful blond angel had just inhabited when Shaw laughed. "I'd let that one go, David."

"Did you see her?" Astor said.

"We saw her," Shaw said.

"And we also saw him," Daly said.

"He's the kind of self-important son of a bitch who could buy his way out of murdering somebody, Davey," Shaw said.

"I'm going to see to it that you get to your room right away tonight," Fargo said to Astor.

"My nursemaid," Astor said bitterly. "Thank you, sister Chloe."

"Your sister did you a favor, kid," Shaw said. "Fargo here's gonna make sure you live to see New Orleans."

"Yeah, and I'll be a virgin when I get there," Astor said.

Shaw yawned. "Right. Well, I'm going to turn in. Now that Mrs. Winthrop is gone, I just don't feel like sitting here and looking at you ugly bastards."

Daly said, "Look who's talking about being ugly. You couldn't get laid with a gun and a bag of gold."

Fargo laughed. He could never quite be sure if those two disliked each other as much as their bantering indicated. One thing for sure, they definitely enjoyed ragging on each other.

"Turning in doesn't sound like a bad idea," Astor said. He yawned, too.

Fargo studied Astor a long suspicious moment. The twenty-two-year-old never went to bed this early.

Astor was the first to stand. He stretched and yawned again. Both times seemed a little theatrical to Fargo. What was the kid planning, anyway? If he hadn't liked Astor's sister so much, Fargo would've gladly walked away. Being a nursemaid wasn't his style, and neither was floating down rivers on steamboats. The kid was old enough to fend for himself. Even when people accused him of murder.

"You ready to go, Nurse?" Astor asked Fargo.

Daly and Shaw grinned. Daly said, "Makes a nice story for a magazine. 'Skye Fargo Was My Nursemaid.' "

"More like 'Skye Fargo Was My Jailer,' " Astor said. There was an acrimonious tone in his voice now.

"I don't like it any more than you do, kid," Fargo said.

5

"But that sister of yours can be damned persuasive when she wants to be."

A slender blond serving girl stopped by the table and began picking up the empty glasses. Her breasts gave her peasant blouse a most pleasing fullness while her colorful skirt lent her hips a provocative richness.

As she leaned over Fargo's shoulder for his glass, she said, "Do you have a lucky number?"

Clever, too, Fargo thought. In addition to being pretty. "Well, my cabin number's twenty-three. Maybe that'll bring me some luck tonight."

"Twenty-three," she repeated. "Yes, that could bring you some very good luck tonight."

And then she was gone.

Shaw, standing up, doing some stretching of his own, said, "You and that girl couldn't have been more obvious if you tried."

"Jealousy," Fargo said with a laugh. "Pure jealousy. Three gamblers who'll be sleeping alone tonight just can't stand the idea of anyone else indulging in some tasty female wine while they scratch and fart in their sleep."

They all left the casino in good moods.

The night was cool, the moon full. They'd gone into the casino around five o'clock. The vessel had still been moving down the vast river. It would keep moving during the night because the bright moonlight on the mile-wide tide would be enough for the pilot to steer by.

The men went on their way, and Fargo wondered again who was out to get Astor. There are people who hate anybody else's success. It becomes a sickness with them, their hatred; they spend much of their time nurturing the envy, the hatred. And then a small percentage act on it. In the case of Astor, his persecutor had figured out a unique way of getting to the young man. Make it look as if Astor was killing any opponent who beat him. Keep it up, and Astor wouldn't be able to buy his way into a game with a sack of gold as big as the boat they were on.

Astor yawned and said, "Nice night."

"Better out here," Fargo said. "I don't know how you fellas can sit in there so long. All the smoke and the noise and the card games. A couple of hours of that would last me for a couple of months. But you're in there day and night."

"Wait'll we get to New Orleans and that big poker game. It'll be a lot worse."

"Your sister's going to be damned mad if I'm not there with you," Fargo said.

"You're probably right about that, but I don't much like being watched over."

"Get some sleep, David. I'll see you in the morning."

Astor said, "I'll bet that serving girl's already in your cabin waiting for you."

"Well, she did say that twenty-three was my lucky number."

Fargo hurried to his cabin, to see if the number would indeed bring him luck tonight.

<h1 style="text-align:center">2</h1>

When Fargo reached the cabin, he found it empty, filled with nothing more than a slight musty smell.

He lit the lamp, sat on the edge of the bed, and started to remove his boots. When the first one hit the floor with a thump, there was an answering tap from outside. Fargo took off the other boot and went to see who was there.

It was the girl from the casino. She stood in his doorway, one hand on her hip, the other on the door frame, and smiled at him.

"I was beginning to wonder if you were in," she said.

Fargo held up the boot. "I was getting undressed."

"Don't let me stop you."

Fargo moved aside to let her into the room. She looked the place over with a critical eye and turned to face him.

"I thought men were supposed to be messy," she said. "The only thing out of place in here is your other boot."

Fargo, being used to living on the trail, liked to have everything in its place. It made traveling easier. He tossed the boot he was holding onto the floor.

"My name's Skye Fargo," he said. "What's yours?"

"Amelia," she said, smiling. "Just Amelia."

And with that she shrugged, allowing the shoulders of the peasant blouse to slip down, revealing the creamy hillocks of her breasts.

"I think I'll get undressed, too," she said, and after that it was a race to see who could shed garments faster.

Soon they were completely stripped. Fargo reached out to touch Amelia's arm, and she came against him, pressing her firm breasts into him, letting him feel that her nipples were hard as pebbles.

"I've never done this kind of thing before," she said.

It was a lie Fargo had heard more than once, and he never contradicted it. If women wanted him to believe he was a special man, that was fine with him. He said, "I'm honored that you picked me out."

"I had a feeling that you were the kind of man who appreciated a woman, and I need to be appreciated tonight."

Fargo pressed against her so that she could feel the erect hardness below his waist put its brand on her stomach.

"As you can see," he said, "I do appreciate you."

"And a lot more than I expected," Amelia said, nudging him back in the direction of the bed.

He took the hint and lay down, pulling her down beside him. He began by kissing the tips of her nipples and then drew each one into his mouth, flicking them with his tongue. Her breath was hot in his ear, and she wriggled beside him as her excitement increased.

He slid his hand down to the patch of wiry hair between her legs and let his finger slide to the center. She gasped and spread her legs slightly, allowing him to ease his finger down along the hairy crevice, gliding gently over her.

She gasped again and reached for his wrist. He thought at first she was going to make him stop his caressing, but just the opposite happened. She was encouraging him to be a bit more active.

Again Fargo took the hint, continuing to suckle her nipples as he stimulated her below. Before long, she was writhing like a snake on a griddle. She started to make little noises in her throat that grew louder as she got more excited.

"Ah, ah, ah," Amelia gasped. "Fargo, Fargo, Fargo."

She raised her hips, straining against his insistent hand, but Fargo wasn't going to let her finish without him. He removed his hand and slid between her legs.

"Oh, yes," she said. "You know what I want. Give it to me now." Her hips jerked.

Fargo didn't make her wait. He touched the tip of his manhood to her slick wet valley, and she grabbed him around the waist, pulling him into her all the way and pinning him there while she twisted beneath him. She started rocking back and forth, slowly at first and then faster and faster as her excitement grew. She released her grip on Fargo, and as he began to thrust at her, she dug her nails into his back.

"Ah, ah, ah," she cried, louder this time, and she wrapped her legs around Fargo, locking her ankles as if to keep him from pulling away too soon.

But Fargo wasn't about to pull away. He could feel his own excitement building, and continued to drive himself deeper and deeper inside her. Amelia groaned in the fury of her own excitement, tossing her head back and gyrating her hips in time with his thrusts. Their rhythmic motion boiled over into a frenzy, as mutual ecstasy washed over them.

After they had finished, they lay quietly for a while, and then Amelia said, "I haven't been that appreciated in a long time."

"I'm glad I was able to help," Fargo said.

Amelia laughed. "I could tell by looking at you that you could. That's why I asked for your lucky number." Amelia settled back on the bed. "Why are you here, anyhow?"

Fargo's little nursemaid task was no secret, so he told her about it.

"That David Astor has quite a reputation."

"It's just a coincidence," Fargo said.

"Maybe, but I've heard some stories about him that aren't very nice. They say he mistreats women and has a terrible temper."

"I wouldn't know about that," Fargo said. Chloe hadn't mentioned it, but that didn't mean it wasn't true. "He seems all right to me."

"And you're going to be with him until he gets to New Orleans?"

"Maybe even longer. It depends on what happens. I'm trying to keep him out of trouble."

"Why can't you just let things take their course? If he's as bad as I've heard, he doesn't deserve your protection."

"I don't think he's that bad," Fargo said, though he was beginning to wonder. "I'd rather not talk about him right now, though."

"Me neither. In fact, I can think of something that might take both our minds off him completely."

"You can?"

"Oh, yes. If you're up to it, that is."

Fargo was up to it, all right. Twice. After that, Amelia left the cabin, and Fargo fell back on the bed. In seconds he was deeply asleep.

3

Trapped in the no-man's-land between sleep and waking, Fargo couldn't decide if the screams were real or part of a dream. He took a moment to orient himself. Fishy smell of hot August river. The Mississippi. Slap of waves against the side-wheeler he was traveling on. Churn of water from the wheel that helped power the boilers.

No, it wasn't a dream. Somewhere nearby, a woman was screaming.

Into his clothes, into his boots, strapping on his Colt, Fargo raced through the door before his gun belt was cinched tight. At three o'clock in the morning, the passenger deck on the side-wheeler was deserted. Stars trembled in a patch of dark sky between two clouds, and the moon cast a faint light at their edges.

The screaming stopped abruptly. Far down the deck, Fargo saw a woman stagger from her cabin and fall against the railing as if attempting to throw herself overboard. Fargo drew his Colt and rushed forward, hearing, on his way, the sounds of people stirring in the cabins as he passed.

The woman's sobs were as loud as her screams had been. She bent over the railing and began to vomit. Fargo hurried into her room. He saw in the darkness the figure of a man on the floor. He grabbed a lamp and turned up the radiance, making shadows dance around the well-appointed cabin.

Death had turned the man into a grotesque piece of statuary. This wasn't an ordinary death. Fargo slowly began to recognize the man. Fred Hollister.

Lucky with women, unlucky with cards, that was Skye Fargo's song. He hadn't won a thing in the game, had been lucky to break even. But he'd been plenty lucky in his room afterward. Hollister had been much luckier with the cards, but all his luck was gone now, and the money he'd won didn't mean a thing to him.

Hollister's blond wife was being comforted by other passengers, so Fargo took the time to look around the room. He had seen the markings of such a death before in his travels. Poison.

When he returned to the deck, he saw the captain of the ship asking the passengers to please return to their cabins. They did so reluctantly. This was a lot of grisly fun, a little something extra for their passage fare.

"Why don't you come to my office with me, Mrs. Hollister?" Captain Titus Montgomery said. He was a tall, somewhat paunchy man with silver hair and a serious manner. He managed to convey official status without seeming stuffy. "I'll fix you some tea and we can talk."

"I know who poisoned him," she said between sobs, daubing at her face with the handkerchief Captain Montgomery provided. "It was that gambler, Astor. David Astor."

Montgomery slid a paternal arm around her shoulders and led her to the staircase. As he was walking away, he looked over at Fargo and said, "You may as well get some sleep, Mr. Fargo. The excitement's over."

11

The captain didn't try to hide his distaste for Fargo, who was impressed that Montgomery remembered his name. Four hundred people on this side-wheeler and the captain seemed to remember each and every name. It was quite a talent.

Fargo nodded in Montgomery's direction, but as he was too jangled up for sleep he took a long stroll around the deck. At the west end of the deck, he saw the crowded mass of scruffy, often dirty, passengers—immigrants, usually—who couldn't afford cabins so slept on the deck. Fargo admired them. Here they were in a new land. They'd had the courage to come to America for the sake of their children. Crossing an ocean in frail, filthy little boats frequently cost lives. A few eyes, glinting in the moonlight, watched as he climbed the stairs to the deck above. He still wasn't sleepy enough to return to his cabin.

The pilothouse was dark, but the pilot would be awake. The other officer would be sleeping in the texas and neither would like it if they knew he was up here. He walked to the opposite end of the deck. Below him was the hundred-foot saloon and gambling casino. Quiet now.

He stood staring at the wake the packet boat left, the turmoil of churning water from the paddle wheel phosphorescent in the light of the moon that was showing itself through a break in the thick black clouds. Fargo thought briefly of the dead man below, but he decided that it wasn't his problem. He was headed to New Orleans where he planned to relax, if Astor gave him the chance. Things like murder he'd leave to the police.

Fargo was just about to go back down the stairs when he saw a shadow-shape duck behind lifeboats stacked three high. The animal in Fargo took over. All his senses came to full life. Eyes, ears, nose alive to the most fleeting sights and subtle sounds and odors.

The shadow-shape was watching him.

Fargo walked to the staircase, descended, and walked quickly across the passenger deck and up the far set of stairs leading to the light hurricane deck.

He walked quietly as a shadow. He wanted to surprise the shadow-shape.

He moved on tiptoe down the deck until he came to a dark tower of stacked crates lashed down tightly with thick rope. The moon had slipped behind another cloud, and the night was so black that Fargo could hardly see three feet in front of him.

He slid his Colt from its holster and waited until he heard a sound that would give him the location of his prey.

The shadow-shape was good at hiding, if nothing else. It hadn't made the slightest sound. If it had, Fargo would have heard it. Nearly five minutes went by.

Then its foot scraped against the wooden flooring. The shadow-shape was nearby, right behind the next stack of crates.

Fargo let another minute go by to be sure. The shadow-shape moved again, enough to shout its location loud and clear to senses as well developed as the Trailsman's.

He slipped around the crates and jabbed his Colt into the stomach of the waiting shape. There was a gasp of surprise and shock, and then a man said, "Goddamn!"

When Fargo heard David Astor's startled and frightened voice, he wasn't surprised. The moon peeked out, and Fargo surveyed the gambler.

If Astor had a gun, he wasn't using it tonight. In fact, he didn't seem to have any kind of weapon at all. He was a big blond man still wearing the standard-issue gambler's clothes he'd worn in the casino—the black sport coat, the brocaded vest—red in this case—the frilly shirt and stylish panama hat.

Astor said, "Please don't tell them you found me. I didn't kill Hollister. I wasn't even near his cabin."

What he should have done, Fargo thought, was poke the gun in Astor's back, march him right down to the captain, and walk clear of the whole thing. But there was something compelling in the simple way Astor proclaimed his innocence. He wasn't overly emotional but each of his words was charged with feeling. Fargo recognized Astor's sincerity. He wasn't given to great drama, either. He was plainspoken and to the point. And he'd many times found himself falsely accused.

Fargo said, "You don't have to worry about me turning you in. I'm the one who's supposed to be taking care of you."

"Messed up, didn't you," Astor said, with a feeble attempt at humor.

"I surely did. You say you didn't kill Hollister?"

"Of course not."

"You have an alibi?"

Astor nodded. "I do." He paused, then said, "But I can't tell you what it is."

"Right now I'm your only friend," Fargo said, "so I want to believe you. But you'll have to do better than that, even for me. Either tell me or I'll turn you in."

"All right," Astor said quickly. "I snuck a woman into my cabin."

No wonder Astor had pretended to be so tired after they left the casino, Fargo thought. He'd had someone waiting for him. Considering his own activities, Fargo couldn't very well criticize Astor for that. He said, "Then she'll testify that you were with her all night?"

"She—can't."

Suddenly, a male voice said, "Who's there?"

A stout man in his officer's trousers and with his chest bare was climbing down from the pilothouse. The moon had ducked back behind the clouds, but that was no help, for the man carried a lantern in one hand. And in the other he carried a pistol.

"Get me out of this, Fargo," whispered Astor. "For Chloe, if for no other reason."

Fargo thought about the times he'd been falsely accused of various wrongs. Maybe that was why he believed Astor. And anyway, would an innocent man be stupid enough to come up with a non-alibi alibi? Yes, he'd been with somebody but she wasn't in a position to help him. He had to be innocent—or a liar. Fargo chose to think the former. It was what Chloe would have wanted him to believe, and he'd promised to look after her brother, so he'd do his best.

"What's going on here?" the officer asked as he approached. Unlike Captain Montgomery, he didn't seem to recognize Fargo.

Astor disappeared behind the stacked crates just as Fargo turned to face the officer. Fargo slipped his pistol into its holster and waited for the officer to move closer.

"I was just out for a walk," Fargo said amiably. "That man being killed and all—just thought I needed a little fresh air before goin' back to my cabin."

"You're not supposed to be up here. And what's so interesting about these crates?"

14

The officer's appearance was made sinister by the way the lantern's light played on the coarse features of his face.

Fargo shrugged and said, "I was just looking between them to see if I could see the shore. See the outlines of the poplars in the moonlight."

"There ain't any moonlight now," the officer pointed out.

"That's why I couldn't see the poplars."

The officer thought about that for a moment, but it was too much for him, and he gave up. He said, "You know a man named David Astor?"

"Afraid I don't," Fargo said.

"He killed a man tonight. We're lookin' for him now."

"Who was he supposed to've killed?"

"He wasn't *supposed* to've killed nobody. He *did* kill a man named Hollister."

"Well, if I see him, I'll sure let you know."

"You do that," the burly man said, watching Fargo suspiciously.

As Fargo nodded his good night, he pretended to cough. But in the middle of the cough, audible if one were listening carefully—and he hoped Astor was—he said, "My cabin."

"You say somethin'?" the officer asked.

Fargo gave the guy his most innocent grin. "Afraid not."

He turned back to the stairs leading down and walked quickly toward them. He didn't want the officer to be near Astor any longer than necessary. Maybe the officer would be overtaken by a hunch and start looking behind the crates.

Fargo hurried past the huddled masses on the deck and went to his cabin.

A slight noise alerted him to the fact that somebody was inside. Fargo drew his Colt, curious. As far as he knew, he had no enemies aboard this boat. He hadn't gotten into an argument, hadn't attracted the eye of a bored wife. He'd been a damned angel was what he'd been. So who'd be gunning for him?

He pushed the door in and quickly flattened himself against the exterior wall. All he'd been able to glimpse when the door swung inward was darkness.

Amelia's voice came from inside the room. "Is that you, Skye?"

Fargo holstered his pistol. Hollister's death and the encounter with Astor must have taken more out of him than he thought. He'd forgotten how he'd spent the hour or so after the card game. But he certainly remembered now.

"It's me," he said, entering the room. "What are you doing back here?"

Amelia lay in the bed, the cover pulled to her neck. Fargo could imagine what she had on beneath it: nothing at all.

"All the excitement on the deck woke me up," Amelia said, "and then I thought about how much you appreciated me, so I came back. You weren't here, but since the door wasn't locked I came on in."

Fargo had to get her out of there before Astor showed up. He said, "I couldn't sleep, either. Don't you think you should get back to your cabin?"

Amelia let the cover slide a bit lower. "Why, Mr. Fargo, if I didn't know better, I'd say you were trying to get rid of me."

"I need all my strength so I can appreciate you tonight."

"Tonight? Isn't this tonight?"

"It's morning. Very early morning. Tonight is when we're going to have dinner in the restaurant."

"Dinner? Really?"

"Really."

"The boys back home never buy me dinner before—" She paused. The covering slid down to her stomach, her naked breasts in plain sight. "That'll be great, Skye." She held his face in her hands and gave him a kiss, her nipples rubbing against his chest as she did so, pole-vaulting his sex drive into action again.

But there wasn't time.

Amelia dressed in the darkness and started to linger. But he walked her to the door, kissed her, and shooed her along. "Six o'clock."

"Six o'clock," she echoed.

A few minutes later, a faint knock sounded on his door. Astor was here.

4

However worried he was, Astor hadn't neglected to bring along a pint of rye for his meeting with Fargo.

After warning him to keep his voice low, Fargo poured himself a drink and listened to Astor start in on a rambling explanation of how he'd been framed and how he had to find out who was trying to ruin him.

"People keep dying after they win money from me," he said. "I know I'm not killing them, no matter what some lawmen might think, so I need to find out who's doing it."

"And why," Fargo said. "Don't forget that. In fact, if you can find out why, you might figure out the who part. Maybe the why is easy."

"A professional gambler makes all kinds of enemies. You beat a man at cards. Or he thinks you cheated him. Or you take his IOU and he decides he'd rather kill you than pay you. Things like that. It could be any number of people."

"You have anybody in mind?" Fargo asked.

Astor took a drink of the whiskey. Then he set the glass on the night table near the bed and said, "I've thought about it a lot lately. Whoever's after me is clever. He's not only going to frame me for murder, he's going to destroy my reputation as a gambler. The last three men I've won big against . . . he's killed each one of them. So it looks like I've done it to get my money back. That magazine article said it was unlucky to play cards with me. That if you won big enough you just might find yourself dead. It's stupid, but people believe it. Now there are packet boats that won't let me play, and there are players who walk out of a room as soon as I walk in. He knows what he's doing."

"So this mysterious somebody is destroying your reputation. And then he's framing you for murder."

"That's right," Astor said. "That's exactly what he's doing."

In the gloom of the room, the whites of Astor's eyes gleamed savagely.

"Well, if he framed you three times before, how'd you explain to the police that you didn't do it?"

"Alibis. I always had good ones. And honest ones. As much as they might have wanted to, and they did, there was no way they could possibly prove I did anything. I have an alibi this time, too, but unfortunately . . ."

"She's married," Fargo said, knowing what was coming and finishing the sentence when Astor's voice trailed off.

"Yes. Listen, Fargo, I don't usually fool around with another man's wife. I don't feel good about it. I've done some rotten things with women, I admit, but not with married ones."

"Mrs. Winthrop," Fargo said, thinking that he should have known after the way the two had behaved in the casino. "Anybody see you?"

"I don't think so. We were very careful."

Fargo sat quietly, thinking things over.

"You need to turn yourself in," he said.

"What? This time I don't have an alibi—or one I can use anyway—and they've already convicted me in their minds."

Fargo said, "We can do it this way. You turn yourself in, and tomorrow, I get your lady from this evening to sign a note saying that she was with you."

"She won't do it."

"Maybe she will if she realizes how serious this is."

Astor sighed. "Somebody even robbed me. What a night."

"Robbed you?"

Astor nodded. "I keep all my important things in a lockbox. Two locks on the damned thing. It weighs fifty pounds. I never thought anybody would just cart it off. But that's exactly what he did." Astor rubbed his face. Yawned. "I guess I'm not built to keep running. I need sleep. Are you sure about that idea of yours?"

"I can't think of anything better."

"Then let's go see the captain and talk this thing over. You'll go with me?"

Fargo smiled. "I'm still not sleepy. I need something to do."

The owners of the side-wheeler sent out monthly letters to the captain with reminders to be courteous, helpful, and reassuring to all passengers. There were detailed instructions on what to say when there were maintenance problems with the boat. There were similarly detailed instructions on how to marry couples, keep a dead body from smelling too bad, and quell rowdiness in the saloon or casino.

The owners wanted to portray their vessels as suitable for "people of all ages and incomes," a safe, pleasant way to travel for drummers and families alike.

They were going to raise holy hell about this murder, but Captain Titus Montgomery could deal with it. He'd have to.

Montgomery stood next to the pilot, gazing out at a dawn sky that was erasing dark night clouds one by one. The two men approaching the cabin from below looked familiar to him. He slowly recognized Skye Fargo, the man who'd been on the murder scene tonight. And then he recognized the gambler, David Astor.

Captain Montgomery said a few words to his pilot and then left in a rush, grabbing a Colt as he did so.

Fargo saw what was happening and said to Astor, "Just keeping walking."

As soon as Captain Montgomery came into sight, his gun hand filled, his face tight and angry, Astor lurched to a stop. "He's got a gun."

"He's the captain. He's supposed to have a gun. He thinks you killed one of his passengers."

"You sure this is the right thing to do, Fargo?"

"I don't suppose you have a better idea all of a sudden?"

"Damn," Astor said, nervously. "I guess I don't."

He started walking again, but he didn't have to walk far. The good captain was soon upon them with his weapon aimed right at Astor's chest.

"I'm taking you into custody," Montgomery said, sounding awfully damned official—too damned official for Fargo's liking.

"Now hold on a minute," Fargo said. "This man is turning himself in voluntarily. And you know why he's doing it? Because he's got nothing to hide. So why don't you give him a little breathing room?"

"I don't like your tone, Fargo," Montgomery said.

"Well, I don't like yours, either, Captain," the Trailsman said. Then, knowing that this was going nowhere, he said, "Why don't the three of us go to the restaurant and have some coffee and talk this thing out?"

"Is he armed?" Montgomery asked.

"No, Captain, he's not," Fargo said patiently. "Well, except for that cannon he's got concealed under his coat."

The grim look on Montgomery's face didn't change. He said, "I'm in no mood for humor, Fargo."

"I don't guess you are. Are we going to the restaurant or not?"

Montgomery thought it over and said, "I'd rather you not be there, Fargo."

"Well, that's the bargain we're making with you, Captain. I bring him in, and for doing that I'm allowed to sit in while you question him."

"What's your interest in this anyway, Fargo?"

Fargo touched his neck. "I've seen too many lynchings, the real kind with a rope and the other kind in a courtroom. I've almost been hanged a couple of times myself. People're supposed to be innocent until they're proven guilty. I just want to make sure that Astor here gets a fair shake. Now why don't you put that damned gun away and let's us go have some coffee?"

Montgomery let his hand drop. He tucked the gun into the top of his trousers. But he didn't look happy about it.

"And you're not going to tell me her name?"

"I wish I could, Captain," Astor said. "But I can't. Like I said, she's married."

"Then you don't have an alibi."

Fargo had said nothing for the past fifteen minutes. He just sipped his coffee in the large, empty restaurant and listened to Montgomery try to pry something out of Astor that the gambler clearly wasn't going to reveal. The cooks and waiters were hurrying about, getting ready for the breakfast rush that would start in an hour or so.

"You knew he didn't have an alibi?" Montgomery said to Fargo.

"He has an alibi."

"It's not an alibi if he can't use it. So he has no alibi."

Fargo sighed. What Montgomery was saying was hard to argue with. Fargo said to Astor, "The captain needs to talk to her."

"No," said Astor, "I don't think she'd talk to him."

Fargo was the one to shake his head this time. "I'd sort of hoped that when I got you in here and sat you down and you were talking to the captain here—I figured you'd tell him her name and what cabin she is in."

"No. I won't do that."

"Then Montgomery here's going to take you into custody. He's got that right as a captain. I imagine we're talking handcuffs and leg irons until we get to New Orleans."

"And the brig," Montgomery said. "We've got a small room we use as a brig."

"That's a hell of a way to get to New Orleans," Fargo said to Astor. "You going to let him do that, or will you tell him who your alibi is?"

"I don't have any choice."

"It'll be the same when they put you on trial, Astor. Unless you produce an alibi, they're not going to look around for any other suspects."

"You can carry this sort of thing too far, Astor," Montgomery said. "There are ways of making discreet inquiries. With this woman, I mean."

Fargo thought the same thing. He was wondering whether he should just go ahead and tell Montgomery about Ida Winthrop. But maybe Astor would do it.

"I have—had—a daughter, Astor," Montgomery said, and something changed in his voice and eyes, something that Fargo couldn't quite interpret. Sadness? Yes, and something else, something hard and secret. "If she was in this sort of mess, I'd like to think she'd help save a man's life."

Astor didn't quite say that he didn't give a damn about the captain's daughter, but it was clear what he was thinking. And he was unyielding in his refusal to talk.

"I'm not giving her name," he said.

"You think she'll come to the hanging?" Fargo said. "I

sure won't. Because even if you are innocent, Astor, you're acting pretty damned stupid."

"I'm wondering if he's even got an alibi," Montgomery said. "Maybe this woman doesn't even exist."

"I think you're right, Captain," Fargo said. "He's a damned liar."

Even under the circumstances, Astor managed a grin.

"You're not going to trick me into telling him who she is, Fargo," Astor said.

Fargo sighed. "Take him away, Captain," Fargo said. "He's all yours."

From the pocket of his uniform coat, Montgomery took a pair of handcuffs.

Astor offered no resistance. He held his arms straight out. The metal cuffs went easily around his wrists.

"I didn't kill that man, Captain," Astor said, "whether you believe me or not."

Montgomery led him away.

<hr>

5

Fargo went back to his cabin and got three good, hard hours of sleep. Then he got some fresh water for washing up and shaving.

It was several more hours before he could isolate the Winthrop woman. As he wandered the deck, he saw the Winthrops heading to the restaurant. Easy to see why Astor had been attracted to her. A slender, pretty woman with the same casual air of sophistication and impudence seen on the faces of society women in Denver and St. Louis.

Cameron Winthrop gave the impression of even greater sophistication and impudence. He wore a summer-weight white suit and carried a gleaming black, gold-topped walk-ing stick that he liked to tap on the deck.

Once he located their cabin—there were four very special cabins isolated from the others for the wealthy and the important—Fargo found a chair to sit in and a newspaper to read.

Wherever they'd gone, they were taking their time. The sun was at midpoint before they appeared. Mr. Winthrop looked drunk; not spectacularly drunk but a little wobbly of knee and wandering of direction. Ida Winthrop kept a tight grip on him.

They went into the cabin and the door closed. Mr. Win-throp was going to nap, but how about his wife? Fargo could spend the rest of the afternoon here and never get a chance to see her.

But then she was there. She wore a lightweight, white walking outfit and had let her blond hair fall loose about her shoulders.

Fargo gave her a minute, then folded his paper and started following her. The decks were crowded. Couples strolled, a man in a rather pretentious painter's smock and beret worked on a canvas depicting the shoreline, and the immigrants on the lower deck basked in the healing and cleansing powers of sunlight.

Fargo wondered where Ida Winthrop was leading him. She had circled the boat twice. Was she confused about her destination or was she simply out for a stroll with no partic-ular destination in mind?

Once, she paused and started to turn her head to look over her shoulder. Had she become aware of him? But then a child ran into her and she didn't complete the turn. The boy had been fleeing his younger brother in a game of pursuit only five-year-olds were smart enough to under-stand. She didn't look back and just started walking again.

After beginning her third trip around the boat, she paused. This time she did look around. But it wasn't as if she wanted to know if she was being followed. It was to see if anybody was around to watch her do what she did next.

And what she did next was to insert a key into the door of David Astor's cabin and let herself inside.

Now why would she do something like that? She had to

know that Astor was under lock and key, presumed to be the killer the ship's captain had been looking for. She also had to know that a lady entering the accused man's cabin would certainly place herself under a certain amount of suspicion.

He sensed that she'd taken all these trips around the boat to work up her courage. What she'd just done was risky. And the law—when the boat docked—would certainly be interested in why a prosperous young woman like herself had gone into Astor's cabin.

He walked to Astor's door and leaned against the adjacent wall. Now waiting wasn't a chore, it was a pleasure. He couldn't wait to see her expression when she walked out of the cabin and saw the knowing smile on his rugged face.

She spent fifteen minutes in the cabin. If she was a thief, she wasn't a very accomplished one. Several times she bumped into things. Once, she even nudged something made of glass and knocked it to the floor. The curses she spewed were almost as loud as the breaking glass.

A few more minutes passed and the door creaked open. She poked her head out—it was a very fetching head—and she saw Fargo and the gun he had pointed right at her face.

"Let's go back inside," he said.

"I will not!" she snapped.

He didn't give her any choice. He filled the doorway and started walking toward her. She had to retreat.

"Sit down over there," he said, indicating the room's only chair.

"I saw you at the poker table last night," she said. "Who are you?"

"I'm the man who knows you spent several hours in this cabin last night with David Astor."

"That's a lie!"

"Is it? Then why did you sneak in here today?"

"That's none of your business."

He surveyed the floor. "You're not used to doing housework, are you, Mrs. Winthrop? You left a lot of broken glass on the floor."

She'd had time to gather herself. She'd looked vulnerable—frantic, scared—for a moment, but now the imperious look was back on her splendid face and she assumed the tone of a queen speaking to a peasant.

"Are you familiar with the word *rape*?" she asked. "All I need to do is start screaming and people would come running."

"And then all I'd need to do is ask your husband if he happened to know where you were late last night, and how we happened to be in this particular cabin."

She sighed, put long, slender hands in the lap of her white skirt. She angled her head so that blond hair covered half of her face. She was the kind of woman that men wanted to capture and hoard, like treasure. Fargo didn't blame Astor for the chance he'd taken.

"I found David attractive," she said quietly. "So I flirted with him and let him think he was seducing me. He's quite a vain man, you know."

"He may be vain, but he didn't kill anybody. And you can prove it."

She lifted her exquisite face to him.

"And just what's your interest in all this?" she asked.

"I've been railroaded myself before. Came damned close to getting hanged for something I didn't do. I hate to see it happen to anybody else."

"You're a lot smarter than you look, I think," Ida Winthrop said. "I thought you were just another ruffian, but it's obvious that you're not. What's your name?"

"Fargo, Skye Fargo."

"Just like the stage line, Wells Fargo."

"Just like that," Fargo said.

She had been trying to smile and keep up appearances, but now she looked suddenly miserable.

"I can't admit publicly that I betrayed my husband," she said.

"Maybe," Fargo said. "Just maybe you won't have to."

"How else can I help David? I'll have to go to the authorities."

"What if I can convince the captain to come here and talk it over with you?" Fargo said. "He could keep it to himself until he talks to the police when we dock in New Orleans. And even then, you and your alibi could be kept quiet."

"No one would know?"

"What'd be the point? I'm sure the police would go along with it."

"All right, then. I'll give David his alibi."

"You wait here. I'll go look up the captain right now."

Before he knew it, she was in his arms. Her perfume made him dizzy, and the slender but tender qualities of her body made him even dizzier. He felt his manhood begin to swell.

"I feel so much better about this," she said and then raised her face to his and kissed him. It wasn't a passionate kiss but it was enough to rattle Fargo right down to the toes of his boots.

"You never did tell me what you were doing in here," he said, as they came apart.

"Simple. I was afraid I'd left something behind. Something that could be traced to me."

"I guess that makes sense."

"It should," she said. "It's the truth."

She sat on the bed and crossed her legs, not quite demurely, so that Fargo got a good look at her quite nice ankles. For the first time he had a hint that she might be putting on a show for her own purposes. The feckless adulteress; the innocent betrayer.

Or maybe he was being unfair. Maybe she was as innocent in her way as she seemed. Maybe she really didn't have trysts with men other than her husband. Maybe she really hadn't been teasing him just now with her seemingly innocent kiss of simple gratitude. Women were harder to figure than the odds on a faro table.

6

Fargo watched Captain Titus Montgomery walking among the passengers on the second deck, applying smiles and little witticisms and even a bit of elbow touching and back patting where it seemed appropriate.

Yes, indeed, we're continuing on our way now to New Orleans and everything is just fine. We have the man who committed the murder, and we plan to turn him over to authorities as soon as we reach the city. So why not relax and enjoy yourselves? Everything is under control. You're perfectly safe, and since we've got almost a full day on the river ahead of us, why not just visit the casino and enjoy yourselves?

For a gruff river man, the good captain was accomplished at spreading on the butter.

Fargo went up to him and said, "Maybe you should run for office someday. You any good at kissing babies?"

Montgomery was not amused. He said, "I don't find you funny, Fargo. I'll be glad when you're off my boat, in fact. The way you dress and your attitude, you should be down there with the riffraff."

"I take it you mean the immigrants?"

Montgomery grimaced. "Call them what you will, Fargo. I don't like having them on my boat, and I've told that to my employers many times. They should be put on cattle boats."

Fargo smiled. "Nobody's ever going to accuse you of having a soft spot in your heart."

"Which doesn't bother me in the least," Montgomery said. "What is it you want, anyway?"

"You know that alibi you said Astor didn't have? He has it."

Montgomery looked surprised. "What're you talking about?"

"Just what I said. I talked to the woman Astor was with. He couldn't have committed the murder."

"And she'll testify to this?"

"We'll meet her in Astor's cabin. She'll tell you about last night. Then you'll let Astor go."

"Oh, I will, will I? On the word of some tramp?"

Fargo laughed. "What if I told you that she's very rich and her husband is very powerful? Would that make a difference?"

"You're making this up, Fargo. I know it."

"See for yourself if I'm lying," Fargo told him. "Come on. We wouldn't want to keep a lady of such high-class breeding waiting for us, now would we?"

27

*　　*　　*

Kenneth Shaw and Robert Daly, in the time-honored tradition of riverboat gamblers, had a little breakfast with their first few drinks of the morning. Not enough to spoil the liquor, just enough to give them a little energy for the long day and night ahead.

Since there were no new newspapers to be had, and since they had no special interest in anything that happened outside their own little world anyway, they talked about the weather and about women they'd like to bed on this trip. When they tired of that, they made quiet fun of the various people who came in and out of the ship's restaurant.

Inevitably, their conversation turned to Astor.

"You don't really think he's been killing all these people, do you?" Shaw asked.

Daly gave it a moment's thought before saying, "I've known him for a good while, and he doesn't seem like the type to kill anybody. But he damn sure has a temper, and I guess you never really know about anyone."

"Maybe it's like Astor says. Somebody's killing all these men because then it'll look like he did it."

"That's a possibility, too," Daly said.

"No matter what, it's fine with us."

A slow, cold smile broke over Daly's face. "That's true." They ordered another round of drinks.

"Astor's a goner," Shaw said when the drinks came. "One way or the other."

"Looks like it," Daly replied without emotion.

"He'll be swinging from a rope within six months. Either that, or somebody will kill him."

"Either one of those things would be terrible," Daly said in the same flat tone. "They certainly would. But I'll drink to them anyway."

Shaw grinned, and they raised their glasses and clinked them together.

The walk to Astor's cabin took three times as long as it normally would. Passengers rushed up to Captain Montgomery with the inevitable questions about the Hollister murder. It seemed that each and every passenger wanted personal reassurance from Montgomery that everything was all right.

"You're a popular man," Fargo said.

"Too popular sometimes," Montgomery said. "I think we've got our man in Astor. He's been on board my ship many times, and he always starts trouble, either with women or cards. But if he doesn't happen to be the man—"

"If he isn't, then the killer is still free."

"Exactly. And I sure as hell can't tell that to the passengers now, can I?"

When they finally reached Astor's cabin, the Trailsman paused a moment, his ear to the cabin door. He rapped twice with his knuckles.

A smug smile had already appeared on the captain's face. Fargo pushed inward on the door. The cabin was empty. Montgomery followed Fargo inside. "I'm afraid your little trick didn't work, Fargo."

"Why would I drag you down here if I didn't think she was here?"

"Oh, she was probably here, all right. But she had second thoughts and ran away."

"Second thoughts about what?"

"Second thoughts about lying. If she lied to me and I still insisted that Astor was our man, then she'd have to lie under oath. I think the word I want is perjury. In case you haven't heard, Fargo, people go to prison all the time for perjury."

"She wasn't lying. She really had spent the time with Astor."

"Then why would she run away?"

"She got scared."

"And because she got scared, she'd let an innocent man be accused of murder? She doesn't sound like a very nice lady."

"I'm not sure she is," Fargo said. He was angry and baffled, ready to confront Ida Winthrop again.

Montgomery scanned the room, then stopped to sniff. "I have to say that's nice perfume you wear, Fargo."

"Doesn't that perfume prove she was here?"

Montgomery laughed. "Not at all. You'd make a terrible defense attorney. A lady's perfume lingering in a cabin? All that means is that somebody was here in the past few hours. She could've been anybody."

Montgomery walked to the cabin door. He put his hand on the knob, then turned his head to look back at Fargo.

"I'm not the judge and jury here," he said. "I'll be in New Orleans for five days. I plan to spend some time at that big poker game. You know about that, of course."

Fargo said that he did.

"Well, that's what interests me. As for the murder, I'll let the New Orleans police take over."

Fargo frowned. "Yeah, you'll let them take over after you've made your case for Astor being guilty."

"What the hell else can I think, Fargo? He drinks too much, he's a troublemaker and a womanizer, and he's been known to be a terrible loser with a very bad temper. I've talked to a few people since I saw you last. I know you're Astor's nursemaid and that you're working for his sister. I'm sure his sister portrayed him as a complete innocent. But ask the other gamblers who work the Mississippi. Long before these recent murders, your boy Astor got into several altercations with men who beat him at poker. And it was always the same story. He accused them of cheating him."

"You saw this personally?"

"Several times. Hell, Fargo, there're two ships that banned him because of his temper. He'd lose to a yokel and then wait for the yokel after the game and accuse him of cheating. And then he'd beat the hell out of the yokel."

Fargo still couldn't believe that Astor was a killer, but obviously Astor was no choirboy.

"He's also bad about women," Montgomery went on, his voice hardening. "He's been in trouble more than once for trying to beat some man's time. You didn't know about that, did you?"

"No, I guess I didn't."

"Every bit of trouble Astor's ever been in, he caused himself. You need to keep that in mind, Fargo."

Fargo shook his head. He said, "That woman I told you about was here, Montgomery. Sitting right there on that bed. She didn't have any reason to lie to me. Hell, she didn't even *want* to tell me the truth. I had to drag it out of her. But she told me, finally, and she gave Astor an alibi."

"Well," Montgomery said, "if she turns up again with this remarkable story of hers, bring her to me, Fargo. I'll talk to her and keep her story private. And if she can convince me she's telling the truth, I'll let Astor go. How's that?"

"That's a deal. I'm going to find her again right now."

This time, Montgomery's smile was actually friendly. "You're a good man to know, Fargo. But this time you picked the wrong friend."

And with that, he gave a little military salute, stepped out onto the deck, and disappeared.

7

Twenty minutes later, Fargo found the Winthrops leaning against the rail, looking at the shore that was growing denser with trees and foliage the farther south the ship took them. At some points, several youngsters appeared, waving at the people on the boat. Most of the waves were returned with smiles.

Mr. and Mrs. Cameron Winthrop looked quite happy and quite married. Every few words he uttered seemed to elicit broad smiles or silver laughter from Ida. And she couldn't seem to grip his manly arm quite tightly enough, clinging to it as a child does a parent. Both in summer white, him in a plantation suit with panama hat, her with a frilly, white silly thing that only a Southern lady could get away with.

Fargo was tempted to go back to their room and break in. He hated to just stand around. But what would he be looking for? Did he think Cam Winthrop might be Hollister's killer? Possibly. Winthrop had most likely heard the stories about David Astor, about the men who'd gotten killed simply for beating him at cards.

Maybe Winthrop had followed his wife to Astor's cabin. And maybe instead of facing off with Astor directly, he'd decided to be clever. Frame Astor by killing Hollister. Then humiliate his wife by forcing her to be Astor's alibi.

Fargo shadowed them on their next stroll around the deck. Every few steps, Winthrop would snap his walking stick against the deck, as if testing the sturdiness of the floor. Fargo didn't know how Ida could stand it.

The Winthrops strode the deck like royalty, she no less than he, and after a while they headed back to their cabin. The shadowing had been fruitless.

Or so he thought.

He was about to turn back to his own cabin when he saw the little girl—clearly an immigrant—come walking quickly toward him. She walked along with brisk confidence, as if she had as much right to be where she was as anyone.

She hurried on past Fargo just as he came to the curve in the deck. He took a last look back at her as he walked around to the next stretch of deck and paused to see what she was up to.

She walked right up beside the Winthrops, looked around calmly, and then took a small white envelope from inside the boyish shirt she wore stuffed inside a worn pair of denim overalls. With a smooth precision that might have been luck or even the result of long practice, she slipped the envelope into Mrs. Winthrop's hand so unobtrusively that Cam Winthrop didn't notice a thing.

The Winthrops continued on their way, and the girl turned and took off running at cannonball speed, straight back the way she'd come, right into the arms of the waiting Skye Fargo.

"Hey, hey, slow down," Fargo said in a gentle voice. "You don't want to break a leg or anything."

"You let me go!" she said sharply.

And then she kicked him right in the shin. Fargo was surprised, and his shin stung from the sharp kick, but he didn't let her go. He held on to her shoulder.

Freckled, scruffy, awfully tough looking for somebody her age, the little girl then let out with a scream loud enough to summon the authorities all the way from Canada.

"Is he bothering you?" asked an elderly lady who hurried along so that she could reach Fargo and the girl.

Fargo decided this was probably a good time to drop his hand from her shoulder.

By then, a couple of men came along. They looked prosperous and concerned. One of them said, "Is this the little girl who screamed?"

"Yes," said the dowager. "He seems to be holding her against her will."

"Where are your folks?" said the second man.

"Down there." The girl pointed to the steerage section on the floor below.

All three faces of the strangers reflected their displeasure. An immigrant girl. Not worth bothering with.

"Then go to them now," said the first man.

"Will you let him hurt me?" the girl asked.

She was all bad-theater mannerisms. The big eyes. The trembling lips. But her stare was pure steel. She was winning this game and she planned to inflict some real damage on Fargo before it was over.

If Fargo hadn't been so pissed, he would've laughed. This was one of the worst ham acting jobs he'd ever seen. And the strangers were, of course, applauding its brilliance.

"She may know something about the killing last night," the Trailsman said. "My name's Skye Fargo and you can ask the captain about me."

"You can be sure that I will," the dowager said. "Now let this poor youngster go."

The girl kicked Fargo again. If possible, this kick was twice as hard as the one she'd planted on him before.

Fargo bent forward, and for just a second he thought his legs might give way under him. They didn't, however, and the three adults clucked their snooty displeasure over his behavior while the little girl ran off. When she was about ten yards away, she turned her head, and seeing that the three strangers had their backs to her, she stuck out her tongue at Fargo.

"You can't trust anybody today," the dowager said.

The men agreed and clucked their tongues at the wickedness of the world as the three went on their way. Fargo heard them talking about him as they walked.

"I'll be having dinner with the captain in a few hours," one of the gentleman said. "And I'll be sure to ask him about this Skye Cargo fellow."

"I think he said 'Fargo,' " his friend said.

"No, no. He said 'Skye Cargo.' I'm quite sure of it."

"Yes," the dowager said. "That's it. That's it exactly."

Half an hour later, Fargo found Ida Winthrop alone at the rail. The river had widened to reveal steep, red clay cliffs on the western shore. Below the cliffs, several fishermen in rowboats waved to the boat while a small group of Indian children stood stoically above them at the top of the cliffs. The river was smooth today. The weather, in the last of the afternoon, was mild.

Ida seemed unaware of Fargo at first. She appeared so deep in thought that she was even unaware of the children charging back and forth on the deck.

"You disappointed me, Mrs. Winthrop," Fargo said.

She turned but didn't seem to recognize him at first. Then her eyes darkened, and she said, "Oh. It's you."

"Yes. Me."

"I'm sorry I disappointed you," she said, not sounding sorry at all. "But I'm afraid things have changed."

Fargo could guess what one of those things was. He said, "Your husband found out about your little transgression."

"No," she said. "He didn't. But somebody else did."

"I'm afraid you've lost me, Mrs. Winthrop."

She had a frivolous little handbag clutched against her stomach. She opened it, reached inside, and pulled out an envelope.

"I received this today," she said.

"I saw who delivered it," Fargo said. "A little girl. Somebody must have paid her to do it."

"Here," Ida said, thrusting the envelope at him. "Read it."

It wasn't difficult to guess the letter's message. Blackmail was common enough. There were people who knew how to learn a night's secrets and how to turn a profit on those secrets.

> I want $2500 cash the day
> we reach New Orleans. Or I
> tell your husband about Astor.

"Whoever sent this doesn't waste any words, I'll say that for him."

"That's all you've got to say, Mr. Fargo? The man's blackmailing me."

"And you're keeping an innocent man in custody. Why did you leave Astor's cabin?"

"I heard somebody on the deck. He kept coming up to the door. Finally I had to know who it was. I yanked the door open but he was running away."

"Any idea who it was?"

"Not really. It could've been anybody."

"Your husband, maybe?"

"I would have recognized him." Her voice was sharp. "And my husband isn't a killer."

"You still haven't answered my question, you know," Fargo said.

"Which is?"

"Which is why you left the cabin."

"I was afraid whoever was outside the door might come back. I didn't want to be there if he did."

That sounded reasonable enough to Fargo. But he was in no mood for letting Ida put off her duty any longer.

"You owe Astor the truth," he said. "You know he couldn't have killed Hollister. Tonight—and I don't give a damn how you do it—you be at the captain's cabin at eight o'clock. I'll have the captain there and you can tell him about last night."

"And if I don't?"

"And if you don't, I go to your husband and tell him what happened."

She received the words like a slap. "You wouldn't."

Fargo grinned. "Sure, I would. I'm Astor's nursemaid."

"That's what I heard. But that's ridiculous. He's old enough to take care of himself."

"Is he?" Fargo said.

She smiled reluctantly. "I guess you'd have to be a woman to appreciate his particular charms. But I guess he is pretty immature."

"You seem to like them that way, Mrs. Winthrop."

"Maybe you're right. I've thought about that myself. The kind of men I'm attracted to—or at least the ones I always end up with—they're always getting in scrapes they can't handle. Somebody else has to save them." She eyed him frankly. "Maybe it's time I started looking for a different kind of man, Mr. Fargo. Somebody who can handle his own trouble. And doesn't need a fortune or a nursemaid to do it for him."

He couldn't tell if she was sincerely offering herself or simply trying to manipulate him, to seduce him into trusting her. He knew better than to play along. So he said, "Captain Montgomery's cabin tonight at eight o'clock. And you'd damned well better be there."

8

For once, the encampment of immigrants looked vital and healthy. People were cleaning themselves in the sunlight from buckets of water. Children were playing and chasing each other around. There was even music from an accordion and a fiddle. Fargo realized for the first time that they were Gypsies.

At first, Fargo didn't see the girl who had tried to break his shins. But then there she was, near the railing, helping a couple of younger girls with a doll so old that the face was worn through in places.

A heavy-set, bald man sat near the fiddler, who in turn sat only a few yards from the shin kicker. Fargo watched as three people took turns coming up to the bald man and whispering things in his right ear, from which dangled a golden earring.

Fargo waited his turn and went up to the man, who was dressed in a red blousy shirt and checkered pants stuffed into calf-high mountain boots. It was hard to say which showed more wear, the man's scarred and battered face or his immense scarred and battered hands.

Fargo watched as the man visibly prepared himself for the Trailsman's approach. The hands became fists. The back arched. The dark eyes gleamed with the promise of much violence should the stranger in any way displease the leader.

"Good day to you," said the leader. But there was neither merriment nor welcome in his thunderous voice. Upon his bald head sunlight danced. "I am Rastin."

Fargo said, "Good day. I wonder if I could talk to you a minute."

"It is the birthday of one of the children," Rastin said. His arm swept in an arc that took in the entire end of the boat. "So we celebrate. This is not a time for business."

The shin kicker was looking at Fargo now. The Trailsman nodded in her direction.

"So you're the one who bothered Duma," Rastin said.

And before Fargo could comprehend what Rastin did, let alone defend himself, he found himself ducking a punch so quick that it announced its speed with a whistle.

The music stopped quickly. The Gypsies gathered to see their leader put the intruder in his place.

"The old ones have a name for men like you, who would steal our children," Rastin said as he circled Fargo. "But it is too foul to say out loud in this company."

"I'm just trying to figure out who killed Hollister last night," Fargo said, backing away. "That girl delivered a message to someone this afternoon. I wanted to find out who gave her the message."

"You frightened her," Rastin said. "And that is not permissible. Not in our code of honor, it isn't."

He was good, and faster than Fargo had bargained for. His booted foot shot out like a rattler striking, catching Fargo in the most tender and vulnerable of all male spots.

Fargo couldn't remember having suffered such pain, not even from a gunshot. He doubled over, forbidding himself permission to cry out in agony, backing away from Rastin's assault.

Rastin landed four punches in a row. The crowd of Gypsies exulted with applause and shouts and taunts. Rastin exulted, too. He even played to the crowd.

"Rastin feels like a young man!" he shouted, thumping his chest and wading into Fargo again.

Fargo fought against his pain. He forced himself to focus, his brain giving sharp commands to his right leg. It was going to hurt like hell to raise that leg, but dammit, he was going to do it even if it killed him. Which he was afraid it might.

But it didn't. His leg shot out, and if it didn't move as fast as Rastin's had, it still managed to catch the Gypsy chief completely off guard.

It also caught Rastin right in the same tender and vulnerable spot where he had caught Fargo, and it caught him almost as hard. The difference was that Rastin kept coming, his arms spread wide as he prepared to seize Fargo the way a marauding black bear would. If he got his massive arms around Fargo, he could squeeze the breath from him as surely as the bear would do.

But Fargo was ready. His own hands were fists now, and he was prepared to keep on fighting through the pain. There would be time later to give in to his misery. That is, there would be time if Rastin didn't squeeze him to death.

Rastin roared his defiance, but at that moment, his brain at last informed his body that a good deal of damage had been inflicted on his testicles.

Pain flooded Rastin's eyes, and he cried out like a gut-shot animal. There was even pain in the way that he clutched himself and began to hop up and down, first on one leg and then the other, in counterpoint to his agony.

Fargo decided what the hell. Rastin had gone below the belt first, so Fargo didn't have to feel too bad about wrapping up this particular little brawl right here and now.

Just as Rastin had waded into Fargo a few minutes before, the Trailsman now waded into Rastin. Six, seven, eight times Fargo hit the older man in the face and chest and belly. Rastin finally had to quit holding his balls and throw his arms up to keep the blows from striking.

There was blood in the man's nose; blood on his lips; blood even coming from his ear. Rastin was a mess. But he was strong of body and strong of will. He hadn't gone down yet. Fargo knew that if he didn't finish this in thirty seconds, the crowd would move in so near that somebody could put a knife in his back.

Fargo threw an uppercut, a smashing right to Rastin's sternum, and then a haymaker that most fisticuff experts would have frowned upon because it left Fargo off balance and open to retaliation. But off balance or not, it worked.

Mainly because there was no retaliation. Rastin collapsed onto the deck of the ship.

Fargo heard, rather than saw, somebody rush up from behind. He swung into a turn just in time, bringing up his Colt directly into the face of a swarthy little man with a knife in his hand.

Gripping the man's wrist tightly, Fargo twisted so hard that a small bone in the man's arm snapped. The crowd gasped at the ugly sound. The man broke into tears and scurried away.

"That little girl over there, Duma, delivered a message to Mrs. Ida Winthrop this afternoon," Fargo said, deciding to keep his Colt in his hand. The pain from below still sent waves of nausea through him, but there wasn't time to give into it. He tried to keep his voice level. "That's all I wanted from her. The name of the person who gave her the envelope. Anything else she said is a lie. Now I want an answer and I want it damned fast. Who knows something about this?"

The people gaped and gawked at one another and then turned as one to face Fargo with looks of complete innocence.

Two gypsies were just now starting to pick Rastin up from the deck. "Leave him!" Fargo snapped, pointing his Colt at them.

Fargo walked over to Rastin and said, "Unless you want to see me beat him even worse, somebody had damned well better tell me who the letter was from."

To demonstrate that he was serious, he raised a foot and aimed it at Rastin's head. His groin still pulsed, even from the slight exertion of this calculated bluff.

"Stop!" shouted a middle-aged man with a rash on his left cheek. His scraggly beard could not hide the rash effectively. "I am Noah. Rastin can't tell you who asked Duma to take the envelope and slip it to the woman, because he doesn't know. But I can tell. I am the man. Somebody stopped me in the darkness last night and gave me money to take the envelope and give it to the woman."

"And you don't know who it was?"

"No." His hands made an imploring gesture. "Believe me, sir. Between the darkness, for it was very dark, and the cowl the person wore, I could see nothing. He spoke through some kind of mask. At least I think he was a man. It could have been a woman pretending to be a man." He looked at his friends. "They will tell you. I cannot sleep so easily. So at night sometimes I stroll the deck. This—creature—stepped out of the shadows beneath a stairway. I never got a good look at him. He even wore gloves so I could not tell anything from the hands. He gave me the envelope and much money and said to give the envelope to the woman sometime this afternoon. I took the money, but at the last minute I was afraid to do it—a Gypsy man approaching a wealthy woman, well, you know what people would think. So Duma did it for me." He turned and pointed to the girl. "She is so innocent and vulnerable, sir, helpless as a kitten in this troubled world."

This guy should write for the ladies' magazines, Fargo thought. He sure knew how to sling the melodrama. And as for Duma being so helpless, Fargo wanted to show him his shin bruises.

"You didn't open the envelope?"

"It is bad luck, sir," the man said. "He—or she—said that I was not to open the envelope under any circumstances. So I gave my sacred word that I would not."

Rastin began a long and embarrassing struggle to his feet. Fargo kept a careful eye on him. Rastin had been badly humiliated, but it was his own fault for attacking Fargo before he knew the facts—and God only knew what he might try to do to Fargo now.

But Rastin surprised him. He said, "I have misjudged this man. I should not have attacked him as I did. I was too hasty, and that is why I pulled back and let him win. Because I was so ashamed of my temper. Otherwise I would have beaten him as I beat all those who oppose me!"

The folk were nice enough to go along with the man, who now looked ten years older than he had before the fight started. And a hell of a lot more pathetic.

"You could have killed him, grandfather!" shouted a lad.

"Nobody can beat you, Rastin!" cried another.

A man close to Fargo whispered, "They wish to keep him as leader. So they lie to him and flatter him. Nobody wants to be leader. Imagine trying to keep all these people in line! And the leader has to do all the fighting. I'd rather just get drunk and have women, wouldn't you?"

A kindred spirit, Fargo thought.

The folk really went all out. They began chanting "Rastin! Rastin! Rastin!" And he in turn gave them a sweeping theatrical bow.

Then, surprisingly, Duma appeared and slipped her arm through Fargo's and said, "I'm sorry I kicked you so hard. You should have seen your face. You looked as if I'd shot you."

The chant continued. Duma stood on tiptoe and kissed Fargo on his cheek and then slipped back to stand among her people and take up the chant for Rastin, who was so peacock-proud of having the job as leader, a job, he didn't seem to realize, that nobody else wanted.

Fargo was soon gone.

As the couple walked toward him, Fargo wondered if his vision had started having a little fun with him.

It couldn't be. No. Impossible.

But it was true.

Ida Winthrop and Captain Montgomery were strolling toward him, talking and smiling as if they were old and dear friends. They were still some distance away, so Fargo leaned against the railing and looked out across the muddy river. What the hell was going on here?

"Good afternoon, Mr. Fargo," Ida said.

"Afternoon," Fargo said.

Montgomery basked in Ida's elegance. For the first time, the somewhat prim captain struck Fargo as a full-blooded male and not just somebody who walked around muttering commands. In Ida's presence, Montgomery had swelled up in pride.

Men and women passed by but none took any special notice of the trio. Even so, when she spoke, Ida Winthrop bent close to say, "I spent half an hour with the captain, Mr. Fargo. I told him the truth . . . about last night."

Fargo was amazed. "About being with Astor?"

"She told me everything, Fargo," Montgomery said. "And I've promised to keep it our secret."

Ida smiled up at the captain. Montgomery did everything but glow, he was so taken with her.

"No one will ever know, Mr. Fargo. And we're on our way right now to set David free," Ida said.

"I owe you an apology, Fargo," Montgomery said, and extended a long hand. His hand was like sandstone, coarse on the surface and hard beneath. "I guess I let my dislike of Astor cloud my thinking. But there are still a few other killings that haven't been solved yet."

"You don't think the same person killed all those people?" Fargo asked.

"Maybe. But, then again, maybe not. Maybe Astor killed others and this killing was completely unrelated."

"That doesn't make much sense."

"It does if you consider the fact that we don't know much about Hollister. A prominent businessman like that is sure to have enemies. You can't disagree with that. And maybe one of those enemies is on this ship. Maybe he decided to take advantage of Astor's reputation by killing Hollister, knowing we'd just assume that it was Astor who did it."

"Please," Ida said, taking Montgomery's arm. "No more talk. Let's go set David free."

The captain beamed at Fargo.

"How can I refuse such a beautiful lady?" he said.

Fargo turned away so that Montgomery wouldn't see the look of disgust on his face.

Fargo was at a table having himself some alcoholic refreshment when David Astor stalked through the open door of the saloon. He looked haggard and rumpled and angry.

"That son of a bitch," he said.

"Which son of a bitch did you have in mind?" Fargo asked.

"Montgomery."

"Well, he let you go, didn't he?"

"Only because poor Ida practically promised to sleep with him."

The bartender came up, took their drink orders, and went away.

"David, you've got to admit your past is catching up to you. The fights, the women, and the threats—you're not exactly angel material."

"That's another thing," Astor said, grabbing Fargo's own shot glass and belting back his whiskey. "I'm getting damned sick and tired of you, too. I'm tired of your nurse-maiding. I don't want you around anymore."

"I promised your sister—"

"I don't give a damn what you promised my sister!" Astor shouted, showing Fargo his temper for the first time. Everyone in the saloon watched him now. The punk with the bad temper being a punk once again. "Who the hell're you to give me lessons in clean living? You're some damned saddle tramp who'd rather spend time with Indians than decent white people, anyway!"

It was just then that the bartender set down the fresh drinks. Astor snapped up his own shot glass and knocked it back.

"You stay away from me, Fargo. Or you'll be damned sorry you ever met me! And that's a promise!"

Ten seconds later, David Astor stalked through the saloon door, turned right, and vanished.

"Someday somebody's gonna take care of that little son of a bitch," the bartender said.

"Yeah," Fargo said, lifting his drink and thinking about his promise to Chloe. "That's exactly what I'm afraid of."

9

Fargo's dinner with Amelia was going along just fine until Daly and Shaw showed up. They both looked trim and prosperous in their frilly white shirts and brocaded vests.

"I see that you've traded your ugly charge for a fairer companion," Daly said after Fargo performed the introductions.

"And I certainly don't blame you," Shaw said with a look at Amelia that stopped just short of a leer.

Amelia didn't seem to mind, but Fargo didn't like it. He wondered what Daly and Shaw were up to.

"We were thinking we might have a word with you, Fargo," Daly said. He looked at Amelia. "In private, if your lovely companion wouldn't mind."

"I don't mind," Amelia said. "I have to go to work now, anyway."

She started to rise, and Fargo jumped up to help her with the chair. She smiled at him as if surprised at his politeness.

"I had a wonderful time," she told him. "Will I see you in the casino tonight?"

"I'll be there, and I'm sure Daly and Shaw will, too. They never miss a chance to trim the suckers."

"That's a terrible thing to say about us," Shaw said, "but we'll certainly be there." He flashed Amelia his most charming smile.

Fargo didn't think Shaw had a chance, at least not with Amelia, but he didn't say so. Amelia just smiled and left them standing there.

"How about a drink?" Shaw said.

That sounded all right to Fargo, so he left some money on his table and joined the two gamblers at the bar, where they had a whiskey waiting for him.

"What was so important to you two that you had to break up my dinner engagement?" Fargo asked them after he'd taken a sip of the whiskey.

"Astor," Daly said. "He told us that he was getting shed of you. That you were out of a nursemaid job as of now."

"He's riled," Fargo admitted, "and I don't much blame him. After all, Captain Montgomery arrested him for a murder he didn't have anything to do with. I guess he thinks I should've done a little more to help him."

"Somebody helped him," Shaw said. "Montgomery let him go."

Fargo didn't see any need to explain exactly what had happened. It wasn't any of their business. He said, "That's what Astor told me. That didn't make him feel any more kindly toward me."

"Was he telling us the truth?" Daly asked. "Is your job over?"

His eyes avoided Fargo, and he looked down at his whiskey glass as if there were something much more interesting in it than whiskey.

Fargo didn't think that his job was any of their business, either, and he wondered why Daly wanted to know.

"What difference does it make to you?" he asked.

"We just don't want to see David get hurt," Shaw said with a notable lack of sincerity. "Did you know he has hardly any money?"

"I know he was robbed. I wasn't sure how much was taken."

"Just about everything he had," Daly said. "Except for what he had on him after the game last night, and that wasn't much, considering how much Hollister won from him. You can guess what people are saying."

Fargo could guess, all right, but he said, "Why don't you tell me?"

Shaw didn't give Daly a chance. He said, "They're saying David killed Hollister because he was broke. He wanted to get his money back."

Fargo thought about that, and he wondered why Montgomery hadn't done more to find whoever it was that had broken into Astor's cabin.

"Hard to get your money back by poisoning someone," Fargo said.

Shaw shrugged and said, "Maybe so, but that's what they're saying."

Fargo looked at Shaw, but just as Daly had done, Shaw avoided the Trailsman's gaze. Fargo wondered again just how much the two men really liked Astor. Maybe they hung around with him for reasons other than friendship.

Just then the calliope music started up, as it did every evening like clockwork, and the steam-powered music floated over the boat.

"The casino's opening," Fargo said, pushing away from the bar. "I think I'll go try my luck."

He saluted Shaw and Daly with his glass, took one last swallow, and set the glass on the bar. He didn't look back as he left, but he could feel the two men watching him.

The casino wasn't crowded when Fargo arrived, but there were a number of gamblers at the tables. One of them was Astor, who was playing with Cam Winthrop and a man

Fargo didn't know. Ida Winthrop was there as well, moving around the table as the men placed their bets, leaning down to whisper something to Astor.

Fargo thought it would be a good idea for him to keep his distance from Astor, at least for a while. He found a table where the players didn't mind having him sit in. He played for an hour or so, breaking pretty much even, while keeping an eye on Astor during the lulls in the game.

Daly and Shaw joined Astor's group not long after Fargo had settled in to play, and after a while Fargo turned the conversation at his table to them, knowing that gamblers often liked to gossip.

"Any of you fellas know Robert Daly and Kenneth Shaw?" he asked after tossing in a hopeless hand.

The man to Fargo's left nodded. His name was John Stanton, and while he wasn't a professional gambler, he was more than good enough to hold his own in any crowd. When he talked, which was seldom, he spoke in a dry, dispassionate voice.

Stanton raised the bet and said, "I know them. Why are you asking?"

"I've been playing a little poker with them from time to time," Fargo said. "They seem like sharpers to me."

"Captain Montgomery doesn't tolerate cheaters," Stanton said.

"They've been asking me questions about David Astor," Fargo said. "I thought they were his friends, but the questions didn't seem very friendly. I naturally wondered why."

The man to Stanton's left, Brad Galton, called Stanton's bet and said, "I can tell you about Daly. I was with him once when he'd had a little too much to drink, and he told me that Astor had visited him in his home once and stolen his wife's affections."

Stanton showed a pair of jacks, and Galton revealed three threes. He grinned as he pulled in the small pot.

Fargo didn't have to ask what Galton's euphemism meant, and he didn't doubt the story. Astor's little frolic with Ida had shown that David didn't mind poaching on a married man's territory.

"As for Shaw," Stanton said, picking up the cards and shuffling them, "he could cheat if he wanted to. He's one of the best card crimpers I ever saw. But he never cheats on a riverboat, or anywhere else that he might run into someone who might catch him. I heard once that Astor accused him of cheating. Astor claimed later that it was all in fun, but I don't think Shaw took it that way."

The men anted up, and Stanton dealt the cards.

It seemed to Fargo that the undertones he'd detected in the way the men ragged on Astor had a strong basis in genuine animosity. Daly and Shaw both had reason to dislike Astor, and although it pleased them to pretend friendship, their questions to Fargo might mean that if he wasn't keeping an eye on Astor, they would take advantage of the situation to do Astor some harm. The questions could even mean that one of them, or both of them, might be responsible for the deaths of the men who won money from Astor.

Fargo continued to play until quite late. Amelia came by the table several times, and Stanton and Galton were amused at her obvious deference to Fargo.

"Seems to me that you're getting special consideration here," Stanton said at one point.

"Some of us are just luckier than others," Fargo said.

"Not necessarily at cards," Galton said, referring to the fact that Fargo was now around thirty dollars in the hole.

"True," Fargo said. "But given a choice, I don't think I'd change a thing."

Galton flipped a chip onto the table.

"Don't blame you a bit," he said.

It was late when Cam Winthrop left the casino, and he wasn't at all steady on his feet. When he tried to tap the floor with his walking stick, the tip skidded and he nearly fell. Astor supported him by grasping one arm, and Ida took the other. Between them, Winthrop left the casino.

Fargo cashed in and left the game, telling the men he'd enjoyed it.

"You playing in that big game down in New Orleans?" Stanton asked.

"You never can tell," Fargo said, and followed Astor and the Winthrops out onto the deck.

Humidity hung in the air like wet flannel, and fog rolled across the wide expanse of the river from bank to bank. Fargo heard the low sound of the boat's whistle over the steady chunking and swishing of the side-wheel as it let other boats in the vicinity know that *The Wanderer* was making its cautious way down the river.

Fargo moved carefully forward, trying to get close enough to hear any conversation that might be going on with Astor and the Winthrops. He had gone only a few steps when he became aware that he wasn't the only one out on the deck.

On a nicer night, one when the stars were shining and the moon was bright, there would have been no surprise in meeting other strollers, but this wasn't a night for seeing the sights or taking the air.

Fargo moved away from the rail and into the darker shadows near the wall, waiting to see if anyone revealed himself. The tapping of Winthrop's cane faded into the distance, and Fargo could hear no sound other than the noise of the side-wheel.

He could have been wrong, but he knew it wasn't likely. At times like this his senses were fully alert, and he wasn't prone to mistakes like that. He waited in silence for a full minute, but there was no further sign of anyone else in the vicinity.

Fargo was about to admit he was wrong after all and step away from the wall when a piece of the darkness moved just at the edge of his vision. He turned his head, and a figure separated itself from the night and glided past him as silently as a shadow. It turned off after going only a few yards, ducking down a stairway to a lower deck where the immigrants and others stayed, the ones not well-heeled enough to afford a cabin.

Maybe he was being too careful, Fargo thought as the figure disappeared from sight. Not everybody on the ship had the same interests he did. And not everyone was out to get some kind of revenge on David Astor. Maybe someone had just left the casino about the same time as Fargo and wanted to get back to where there were lights and people.

The side-wheel splashed and Fargo heard Ida Winthrop's voice. He hurried to catch up. He was curious to see if Astor and Ida would deposit the drunken Winthrop in his cabin and set out on adventures of their own.

But Fargo never got a chance to find out anything of the

sort. He made the mistake of letting his guard down and believing that the figure who had gone to the lower deck intended to stay there. Whoever it was hadn't been following the Winthrops or Astor. He'd been following Fargo and had slipped away when he realized that Fargo was on to him.

Fargo heard a step behind him, started to turn, and was struck on his right shoulder with a heavy stick. Fargo's arm tingled from shoulder to wrist. He tried to move it, but it was paralyzed.

Fargo couldn't raise his arm to defend himself, and he couldn't go for his gun. He backed away from his attacker, but the heavy stick hit him again, an overhand blow this time that barely missed his head but again struck his shoulder.

Fargo bit back a cry of pain and kicked out with his left foot, catching the club-wielding figure on the leg. The man stumbled backward and Fargo moved toward him, trying to catch him with a left hook to the jaw. He connected, but the punch was deadened by something the man was wearing. A hood, Fargo thought. Wasn't that what the man who had given the letter to Noah had been wearing?

Before Fargo could remember the answer, the club struck him again. Except that he realized it wasn't a club. It was probably a walking stick, like the one Winthrop affected, but it was being used for a much more deadly purpose.

The stick swished through the air again, but it missed him by a wide margin this time. The hooded man advanced, swinging the stick, but Fargo kept moving away, just out of reach. He tried to see the man's face, but there was nothing but blackness under the hood, and Fargo remembered something else that Noah had said: the man who gave him the letter had been wearing a mask.

Fargo wanted to know who was under the mask, and he wanted to know who was trying to turn him to jelly with the stick that was moving so fast he could barely see it in the fog. He ducked beneath a particularly vicious blow and reached up toward the mask with his left hand. His fingers clutched black cloth just as the stick jabbed him hard below the sternum.

Fargo's breath whooshed out and the mask tore away

in his hand. The stick poked him again, and he stumbled backward. The quick, hard jabs came one after the other, forcing Fargo to keep moving. He dropped the cloth and grabbed at the stick. His fingers closed around it. It was round and tapered, and Fargo pulled the dark figure to him, trying to get a look at the face under the hood. But the night was too dark and the fog too thick for that. All Fargo got was the impression of a pale gray face without features, like a lump of bread dough.

Fargo gave a sharp twist, hoping to wrest the stick from the figure's grasp, but the man managed to hold on. And he quit jabbing. He simply thrust the stick into Fargo's midsection and pushed with all his strength.

Fargo felt the deck railing at his back, his feet slipped, and he tipped over. The figure jerked the stick away from Fargo's fingers and jolted the Trailsman under the chin. Fargo's teeth clicked together as he flipped over the railing, and then he was falling, with nothing to catch him except the muddy water of the Mississippi.

Fargo wouldn't ordinarily have been worried about a little dip in the river. He was a good swimmer, even if his clothes were sodden and even if he had his boots on.

But this wasn't an ordinary situation. His right arm was partially paralyzed, and that was bad enough. What was worse was that he was falling into the path of the side-wheel, which had enough power to break up rafts and small boats and turn them into kindling.

Fargo didn't like to think what it might to do a man.

And then he hit the water, and it was too late to think.

10

The water was warm and thick as soup, and Fargo sank in it like a sack of rocks. His right arm was practically useless, and he struggled to kick his way to the surface. He didn't make much headway, and he could feel himself being drawn toward the side-wheel, which created a powerful current as it turned slowly around. If Fargo didn't break away soon, he was going to be sucked into the wheel and cracked open like an egg.

And there was another problem. If he didn't get to the surface, he was going to drown. The only consolation was that if he drowned fast enough, he wouldn't feel anything when the wheel crushed him. Unfortunately, this didn't seem like much of a comfort at the moment.

He could feel the vibrations of the wheel, and he knew he couldn't be more than a few yards away, though it was far too dark to see anything in the water. He reached out desperately with his left hand, hoping to grab hold of something—the side of the boat, a floating log, a giant catfish, anything. But he grasped only the muddy water that flowed through his fingers and left him holding nothing at all.

Fargo wasn't the kind of man to give up. As long as he had breath in his body, he would keep struggling. He didn't see much hope this time, but he continued to kick his feet and pull himself upward with his left arm.

Just as his lungs were about to burst, his head broke the surface. He shook his hair out of his face and gulped in air. He could hear nothing but the sound of the side-wheel, which continued to draw him steadily toward it.

Fargo tried to swim away from the wheel, but he made

no progress. It seemed inevitable that he would eventually be pulled in.

While Fargo was contemplating his fate, something struck the water only a few feet away. The Trailsman whirled around in the water to see what, or who, it was, but nothing was there.

Then a strong hand grabbed him by the ankle and pulled him down. He started to fight back, but he could do no more than take a deep breath of air before his head was jerked beneath the river's black water.

He was pulled down and down, straight to the muddy bottom. When he reached it, powerful arms held him there, and his feet sank into the gooey mire. Overhead the side-wheel churned the water, and the force of it pushed Fargo even deeper into the mud like a huge hand atop his head.

Fargo didn't know how long he stayed there, but he soon felt as if someone had lit a fire in his chest, which threatened to burst open and spew his lungs out into the Mississippi. Before that happened, however, thick fingers grasped his hair and pulled him upward. Fargo knew what to do then, and when his feet came free of the mud, he kicked as hard as he could. This time when his head popped through the river's surface, the boat had gone by, and the wheel's force was channeled in the opposite direction. Fargo gulped down air, and the current pushed him farther and farther away as the boat drifted slowly downriver.

The fog was so thick that Fargo could hardly distinguish the dim outline of *The Wanderer*. He could hear the mournful tone of the whistle, but he could see neither bank of the river. It was like being lost in a watery desert, and in moments the fog closed around the boat, leaving Fargo completely alone.

Except for the one who had saved him. A hand touched his shoulder, and a voice said, "Do not be afraid. I will get you back to the boat."

"Rastin?" Fargo said, treading water. "Is that you?"

"It is Rastin, indeed. And you are Fargo?"

"Yes. I thought you knew."

"I saw a man fall, so I naturally thought I should save him. I did not know it was you."

Something in Rastin's tone sounded a bit sorrowful to Fargo, as if, having discovered who he had saved, the

Gypsy might now be regretting his decision to jump into the river to perform the rescue.

"But come," Rastin said. "We must swim strongly or we will not be able to catch the boat."

"I can't swim strongly," Fargo said. "My arm's hurt."

"Even so, you must try your hardest."

Fargo tried his hardest. To his surprise, his arm responded better than he thought it would. Even though it hurt every time he moved it, he could almost get the full range of motion from it. He started swimming in what he hoped was the right direction, with Rastin beside him.

It occurred to Fargo that it wasn't very likely that he and Rastin would be able to catch the riverboat, but it was moving unusually slowly because of the dense fog. Before long, the sound of the boat whistle was definitely closer, and Fargo's right arm was feeling stronger with each stroke. To his right, Rastin was swimming determinedly, and sooner than Fargo would have thought, he was able to make out the spectral outline of the boat.

Rastin stopped swimming and touched Fargo's arm. The Trailsman stopped as well, and Rastin said, "There will be a rope. Stay close to me."

Fargo didn't ask how Rastin knew about the rope. When a man saves your life, you have to trust him, at least for a little while. He followed the Gypsy's lead, and when they caught up to the boat, Rastin called out.

"Noah! Noah! Are you there?"

"I am here," a voice answered.

"Throw out the rope," Rastin said, and it splashed into the water in front of them.

"Take hold," Rastin told Fargo. "Noah will pull you to the boat. Then throw the rope to me."

Fargo did as he was told. When he grabbed the rope, he was pulled smoothly through the water, and when he reached the boat, he climbed the rope for a couple of feet. He thought his right arm would give out, but before it did, a hand reached down and pulled him the rest of the way onto the deck.

"Thanks," Fargo said.

Noah said that Fargo was welcome. He pulled in the rope and threw it back to Rastin.

Fargo sank back onto the deck, letting the water run off

his body and pool beneath him. He was tired but glad to be alive.

Rastin pulled himself over the railing and shook off water like a wet dog. Droplets flew everywhere.

"I owe you one," Fargo said, sitting up.

"That is not true," Rastin said, and again Fargo detected that note of regret in his voice. "Now that I have saved your life, I am the one responsible. I must see to it that you do not come to a bad end."

Fargo grinned in the darkness. "That won't be an easy job."

"I do not want to hear about it. I have enough troubles as it is."

Fargo could imagine. He said, "I'm glad you jumped in after me. You didn't happen to see the fella who pushed me, did you?"

"You fell from the deck above. I saw only a body falling, and I told Noah to get a rope. Then I jumped, too."

"I'm glad you did." Fargo ran his hands through his hair, squeezing out water. "I don't think I'll need another bath for a year."

"Were you fighting again?"

"I guess you could say that. It wasn't my choice, but then it wasn't my choice to fight you, either." Fargo paused, thinking of Noah, who was standing silently in the dark beside them. "You had me beat, you know."

"I know," Rastin said. "But because I had misjudged you, I had to allow you to win. Now I have saved you for a second time. Fate must have some important thing for you to accomplish before you meet your end."

"I don't know how important it is," Fargo said. "I'm just a nursemaid to a gambler."

"Do people often try to drown nursemaids?"

Fargo said, "No, they don't. I guess there's a lot more going on with this particular gambler than I realized." He stood up. "And if I don't get back on his trail, there's no telling what might happen to him."

"Do you want me to go with you? To watch behind you?"

"I don't think you need to do that. I have a feeling that nobody's going to try to hurt me again. Whoever did it probably thinks I'm already dead."

"Then it should be interesting to watch the faces of your friends when you meet them the next time," Rastin said. "Come, Noah. Let us go back to our people."

"Thanks again," Fargo said, but they melted into the darkness without another word.

Fargo figured he had lost too much time to bother looking for Astor and the Winthrops. Whatever they were going to do, they'd already be doing it, and most likely doing it behind locked doors. Besides, after his adventure in the river, Fargo didn't feel up to doing anything that required thought or exertion.

He headed for his own room, being careful in the fog and wondering why someone would have wanted to do him in. The obvious thing that came to mind was his connection to Astor.

And then there were the Gypsies. What if one of them was resentful of Fargo's beating of Rastin? He might have tried to kill him to get revenge for his leader's humiliation. That might explain how Rastin had happened to see Fargo's fall. On the other hand, maybe it was just a coincidence, as Rastin had said. That was what Fargo preferred to think. The hood and mask worn by his attacker indicated that the man—somehow Fargo couldn't believe it was a woman—was the same person who had written the blackmail message to Ida Winthrop. That brought things back to Astor again, but it didn't narrow the list of suspects much.

Or maybe it did. Gypsies had the reputation for being partial to easy money earned in nefarious ways. Could it be that Rastin was the one who had threatened Ida?

It was all too complicated to think about, at least by a man who wasn't exactly in the peak of condition. What Fargo wanted to do was get a good night's sleep and get over the effects of his dunking.

He might have been tired and wet when he got to his cabin, but he was still alert enough to realize someone was inside. It was beginning to seem that every time he left his cabin at night, someone was in it when he returned. He was going to have to do something about that.

He'd planned to dry and clean his pistol before going to sleep to avert the effects of the river, and he knew the powder was too wet to fire. Maybe whoever was in the room didn't know that, however. He half-expected that Amelia might be in his bed again, but he didn't want to take the chance. He pushed the door open and went inside, the pistol pointed straight in front of him.

"I really don't think you'll need that," Ida Winthrop said.

"Maybe not," Fargo said, peering into the darkened cabin. "But maybe you'd better tell me why you're here before I make up my mind."

Ida was sitting in the cabin's only chair, and Fargo could barely see more than a dim outline. He recognized her only because of her voice.

"I don't think I want to tell you," she said.

"Then you'd better leave," Fargo said.

"Why don't I show you why I'm here," Ida said, getting out of the chair and walking over to where Fargo stood, stopping when the barrel of the Colt touched her stomach.

"That's cold," she said, and it was then that Fargo realized she was completely naked.

11

"Now do you know what I'm doing here?" she asked.

"Maybe," Fargo said. He was sure he'd locked the door before going to the restaurant with Amelia. "But what I really want to know is how you got in."

"Captain Montgomery came with me and unlocked the door. I told him I wanted to explain a few things to you, then persuaded him to leave."

Fargo didn't ask how she persuaded Montgomery because he thought he had a pretty good idea. He said, "But you don't want to explain anything to me, do you?"

"No. I had something else in mind, and I don't think it requires an explanation."

Fargo knew what she had in mind, all right. He could see her better now, even if not entirely clearly, and her large firm breasts stood up proudly. Her waist was trim, and her hips broadened out from it in a beautiful roundness. Heat came off of her as if she were lit by a fire inside. Even though he'd just nearly been drowned and broken apart by the side-wheel, the Trailsman felt part of himself growing large and thick.

"I'm not the only one who wanted to see you tonight," Ida said. "There was some very annoying knocking at your door earlier. I think it was that woman from the restaurant."

Amelia. She'd probably wonder why he hadn't let her in. Well, he could tell her about his fall overboard. That should cover him.

"You're awfully wet," Ida said, reaching out to touch Fargo's arm. "Is it raining?"

"It's just foggy."

"You didn't get that wet in the fog, did you?"

"No," Fargo said, but he didn't explain.

"You should get out of those damp clothes," Ida said. "You could get a case of the grippe if you don't dry off. And you might put down that pistol, too."

Fargo had forgotten that he was still holding the Colt against Ida's midsection. He was about to lower it, but she reached for it, cupping the cylinder in her hands and sliding the barrel between her breasts.

"Ummmm," she sighed. "That's very hard. It gives me chills." She moved the barrel up and down a few times. "But it's cold. Think how much better something warm would feel."

Fargo holstered the pistol and began undressing as fast as he could.

Ida moved to the bed and watched him.

"I've wanted you ever since I saw you in the casino," she said. "I should never have gone with David, but he was so young and eager that I couldn't turn him down. It was a mistake."

"What about your husband?" Fargo said, shucking his pants.

"Cameron is wonderful in some ways, but he's seldom much use to me at night. You must have noticed how much

57

he drinks. I practically had to pour him into bed tonight. It's that way most nights."

Fargo was thinking that Winthrop was a fool, but he didn't bother saying it. Ida probably knew that already.

"He'll sleep late," Ida went on. "He always does. When he wakes up, he won't remember a thing about tonight, and all he'll want to talk about is the evening, when he can gamble again. That's why we're going to New Orleans, you know. For the gambling. There's a big poker game there that he will be playing in."

"He won't do well if he drinks too much."

"I know that, and I suppose that Cameron must, too, but it doesn't seem to deter him. What's deterring you, by the way?"

"Not a thing," Fargo said, standing beside her as she lay on the bed.

She reached for him and took hold of his stiff penis.

"That's even better than I expected," she said, letting her fingers glide along its length. "Come here."

She pulled him closer and then, taking a firmer grasp, indicated that she wanted him to straddle her. He did so, and she slid his thick shaft between her breasts.

Fargo massaged her melon-sized breasts, pressing them around his pole.

"Oh, yes," Ida said. "That's very warm, much nicer than the gun barrel. Longer, too. And harder. Oh, yes."

Fargo let his shaft slide up and down between the soft, creamy mounds, and Ida sighed. After a moment she reached around him with her right hand, and Fargo could easily imagine what she was doing with it.

"Don't stop, Fargo," she said. "Don't stop."

Fargo felt her moving under him, her hips bouncing and twisting. As she did so, her engorged breasts seemed to take on a life of their own, embracing Fargo's stiff member in elastic warmth as he moved his hands over them. Her nipples, already rigid, extended themselves even farther, and Fargo let his fingertips play and caress them lightly. They felt like glowing coals. He bent down and touched his tongue to one and then the other, licking over and around them. Then he took one into his mouth and sucked it as Ida squirmed and urged him not to stop.

"Put it in me," she moaned. "All the way. Let me have it all."

She didn't have to ask him twice. He slipped between her bent knees and touched the tip of his manhood to the wiry hairs that lined her sweet mound. She grasped him and shoved him inside. But she didn't let him go. She moved him in and out until he was as slick as she was. She opened her legs wider and wider to take him deeper. When she was at the peak of excitement, she wrapped her legs around him as she pulled him into her as deeply as possible. Then she locked her ankles, holding him tightly as she writhed enthusiastically. Her excitement built again, and she loosened her hold. She said, "Now give it to me, Fargo!"

Fargo gave it to her with an enthusiasm that matched her own. No one would have believed that only about half an hour before he had been near to drowning or that his arm had been practically paralyzed.

"Oh, yes yes yes yes yes yes!" Ida moaned.

She bucked and wriggled and twisted, and finally Fargo could hold back no longer.

When they were done, they lay together on the bed, and Fargo wondered why she was really there. Sure, she'd enjoyed the sex as much as he had, maybe more if that was possible, but Fargo didn't for a second believe she'd come there just for that. Fargo had known more than one woman like Ida, and they always had another reason hidden below the apparent one.

"You're a very forceful man," Ida said after a few moments. "And you know how to pleasure a woman."

First the flattery, Fargo thought. Then she might get around to letting him know what she really wanted. He said, "And you know how to pleasure a man. If I were any more pleasured, I'd be dead."

Ida laughed quietly and rubbed her breasts against him.

"If only I weren't married to Cameron, I could have a real man. Someone like you."

So that was it. She was tired of her husband and looking for a replacement. She couldn't just leave him, however. She was the kind of woman who needed a man, preferably a man with money. Astor hadn't worked out. He was in

59

too much trouble, and maybe that was why she had been a little hesitant to help him. There might be too much suspicion of him, and of her, if anything happened to her husband. So Astor really couldn't do much for her.

On the other hand, Captain Montgomery could. She must have made some proposal to him, which would explain why he was so friendly to her. And just in case he didn't work out, she was now trying to beguile Fargo.

But Fargo didn't like being beguiled.

"I've always believed that marriage is a sacred bond. I wouldn't want to be the one to break it."

"What do you call what we've been doing?"

Fargo had no qualms when it came to sex. He had made it a practice never to turn down what was offered to him, whether the woman who offered it was married or not.

"We might have bent something," Fargo said, "but I don't think we broke it."

"But I thought you could help me. I'm married to a weak man who doesn't really love me. And there's the little matter of that letter. We reach New Orleans tomorrow. What am I going to do?"

Fargo didn't think she was really very worried about the letter. If she were, she wouldn't be where she was, doing what she had just done. And there was no reason for her to be worried, Fargo thought. The man who had pushed him into the river was probably the one who'd written the letter. He was interested in hurting Astor, not Ida, although it was possible that he might have been following her to demand his money.

"Have you heard any more from that letter writer?" he asked.

"No, I haven't, but then I didn't expect to."

"You don't have to worry about him. All he wanted to do was scare David, and the murder business took care of that."

"How can you be so sure?"

"I can't. You'll just have to wait and see what happens."

"But Cameron won't be happy if he finds out about David." Ida smiled. "Or you, for that matter."

Fargo wasn't sure he believed her. Besides, after getting to know Ida a little better, he thought she was perfectly capable of handling Cam Winthrop, no matter what he was told about her behavior.

"Is that a threat?" he asked.

"Of course not. I'd never threaten you. It's just that I need to do something about my husband."

"What do you want me to do? Kill him?"

Ida gasped. "Of course not! I'd never suggest such a thing!"

Like hell she wouldn't, Fargo thought. He said, "Good. Because I'd never do a thing like that. What's the real problem? Is he out of money?"

"You bastard." Ida got off the bed and started putting on her clothes. "I thought you were a man, but you're nothing but a coward."

"If you say so," Fargo told her, leaning back and relaxing. "But I'm not a murderer. Neither is Astor, as you probably found out. Those stories about him are pure moonshine."

"As if I cared. Good night, Mr. Skye Fargo."

She went out of the door, slamming it behind her. Fargo smiled up at the ceiling and closed his eyes. It didn't bother him at all that the door wasn't locked. Within seconds he was sleeping soundly.

12

When *The Wanderer* arrived at the dock in New Orleans, it didn't create nearly the excitement it had in the small towns upriver, where it had seemed to Fargo that everyone in town, along with all of the dogs, and sometimes one or two of the hogs, had turned out to greet the steamboat. Its arrival was the highlight of an otherwise dull day.

Here at the levee outside of New Orleans, however, *The Wanderer* was just one among many. Boats lined the levee, which was covered with people, all of whom had much more urgent business than to gawk at *The Wanderer*. Stevedores were everywhere, loading and unloading, and wharves and warehouses were full of goods: cotton, bale after bale of it; barrels full of rum and flour and pork; stacks of animal skins; and coffee. The powerful smell of the coffee mixed with the smells of decaying fish, stagnant water, and rotting vegetable matter. Above all the commotion, the clouds were thick and low and threatened rain, though there was no thunder.

Passengers and visitors swarmed over the levee in colorful clothes, and it was a wonder to Fargo that they weren't walking all over each other. As it was, there was plenty of pushing and jostling. The people were almost as colorful as the clothing. They were black and white and every shade between.

Away from the boats, the passages were lined with stands selling fruit or oysters. They were doing a good business, but not nearly as good as the saloons, some of which had lines of men waiting for that first drink on shore or the last one before getting back on the river. Crowding in among them were men selling flowers and women selling coffee by the cup. Children whirled and danced in hopes of getting a penny for their efforts. A blind man with a rag tied over his eyes played a fiddle, its case open in front of him on the ground if anyone liked his playing enough to offer a reward.

Mule-drawn drays moved among the throngs, their wheels clattering on the stones, and people either moved out of their way or got run down. The drays headed into town were loaded with goods. The drays coming the other way were empty, waiting to be filled. There may have been some order and purpose in it all, but Fargo found it hard to tell.

He also found the noise almost unbearable. He was used to the quiet of the West, where a man could hear a honking gander for miles as it crossed the clear blue sky. Here, he could hardly hear himself think because of the cries, shouts, boat whistles, creaking lines, and the thud of cargo hitting the dock.

When *The Wanderer*'s landing stage swung down, Fargo stood at the rail on the second deck, watching the passengers disembark. The humidity wrapped around him like a wet sheet. His clothes clung to him and mosquitoes buzzed around his head and nipped him here and there. He hoped to catch a glimpse of Astor before the young gambler disappeared into the colorful mob, but he wondered how long he could stay on deck before his blood was drained away.

Fargo noticed that the immigrants were first off the boat, as if eager to start their new lives. He saw Rastin and Duma in the crowd and waved to them. They waved back, smiling, and Fargo hoped that they would have a good life in New Orleans. He watched them as they mingled with the crowd, and he saw Duma slip her nimble fingers into a woman's half-open bag and come out with something she gave to Rastin.

The Gypsy leader looked back over his shoulder and smiled at Fargo, who knew he didn't have to worry about the Gypsies any longer. They were going to do just fine in New Orleans.

Fargo didn't see Astor, but Daly and Shaw left the boat together. Each man carried a small valise, and Daly had another bag that might have held a shotgun or rifle. Fargo wondered if one of them had knocked him into the river last night. If so, they showed no signs of remorse.

Cam and Ida Winthrop were also leaving. They had no bags, but that didn't surprise Fargo. He knew they would have someone else do the work for them. Ida clung to her husband's arm and anyone seeing them would think that they were as happy as any married couple anywhere. Hell, for all Fargo knew, maybe they were. It seemed obvious that whoever had written Ida the letter had not followed up on it.

Fargo was swatting at a mosquito when Amelia came up to him and said that she'd tried to check his lucky number the previous evening. She had to raise her voice a little to be heard over the din below.

"I knocked at the door," she said. "But you wouldn't let me in."

"I wasn't there. I had a little trouble and couldn't get back to my cabin. I'm sorry I missed you."

"What kind of trouble?"

"It doesn't matter. It's all over now."

"What about your friend, Mr. Astor? Will you be seeing him again?"

"As a matter of fact," Fargo told her, "I'm looking for him how. But I don't see him anywhere."

"I'm sure he'll be here. Will you be playing in the big poker game?"

"I'll be there if Astor is."

"Maybe I'll see you, then. I hope so."

"So do I," Fargo said, and she left him with a smile.

She was replaced almost immediately by Captain Montgomery.

"I'd like to have a talk with you, Fargo," the captain said. "In my cabin."

"I'm looking for somebody," Fargo said. "I wouldn't want to miss him."

"Astor?"

"That's right. My job isn't over just because we've come to the end of the line."

"This has something to do with your job. I think you'd better come with me."

Fargo took another look at the disembarking passengers. There was no sign of Astor. Maybe he was still in his cabin. Fargo said, "All right. But I can't stay long."

"And I won't keep you long," Montgomery told him, turning away and heading toward his cabin without looking back to see if Fargo was following. Fargo picked up his bag and went after him.

When they arrived at the captain's cabin, Fargo was about one step behind. Montgomery opened the door and went inside, holding the door open for Fargo, who walked past him into the room. Montgomery closed the door and shut out some of the din.

The room was larger and more comfortable than the one the Trailsman had occupied, and there was even a painting on the wall, a scene showing mountains that Fargo didn't recognize, which he reckoned meant they were in some other country. Either that or they were in the East, an area Fargo preferred to avoid. On the washstand, along with a large glass pitcher and bowl, there was a daguerreotype of a young woman who looked vaguely familiar.

Montgomery saw that Fargo was looking at the picture and said, "My daughter."

"She's very pretty," he said.

"She was," Montgomery said flatly. "She's dead now."

"I'm sorry," Fargo said, remembering that Montgomery had mentioned the daughter earlier. "You didn't ask me here to talk about her, I'm sure."

"No. I want to talk to you about Ida Winthrop."

That was a topic that Fargo would just as soon avoid. He said, "What about her?"

"I know most of what goes on aboard this boat," Montgomery told him. "Especially when it's going on right under my nose. So I know about you and Ida. She didn't fool me for a minute with her story about wanting to clarify some things with you. I know she met you in your cabin last night."

"Do you know that someone pushed me overboard?"

"What?" he asked, surprised.

"I said, somebody tried to kill me last night. I was attacked and pushed overboard."

"If that's true, why didn't you report it at the time?"

"I was tired and hurt, and there wasn't really anything to report. Because of the fog, I didn't see who pushed me. Besides, I needed some rest, and I didn't think there was anything you could do about it."

"You don't look tired or hurt."

"I had a good night's sleep," Fargo said, thinking that he hadn't really had much sleep at all, not that he minded. Ida had been worth it. "And I recover fast. Anyway, you didn't finish telling me what it was you got me in here for."

Montgomery gave Fargo a wolfish grin. He said, "I think you should stay away from Mrs. Winthrop. I know she paid you a visit last night, and I'm not going to hold that against her. Or you, either. But if you see her again, you'll have to answer to me."

"I don't answer to anybody except myself," Fargo said.

He turned and left the cabin. Montgomery didn't try to stop him.

Fargo wondered about Montgomery as he went on his way. As far as Fargo could tell, there had been virtually no investigation of Hollister's death, and none at all of the theft of Astor's money. Fargo thought that Montgomery should have done more, but then the Trailsman didn't know who had jurisdiction on the boat. Was it Montgomery, or some land-based authority? Fargo was out of his territory and couldn't answer the question. He figured it didn't matter anyway because the steamboat company would most likely hush up the murder. Maybe they'd pay Mrs. Hollister a little money to soothe her feelings and to encourage her not to talk. It wouldn't look good for the company if word got out about a passenger's murder. And they'd keep the theft quiet, too, if they could.

Nearly everyone had left the boat by the time Fargo got to the landing stage, so wrapped up in his thoughts that he almost bumped into David Astor.

"Watch where you're going, Fargo," Astor grumbled.

"Didn't see you. Are you ready for the big poker game?"

"That's not any of your business. I told you that I wanted you to leave me alone, and I meant it."

Astor pushed by Fargo and out onto the wobbly landing stage. He crossed it and mingled with the motley crowd. Fargo watched him go. It didn't matter whether Astor wanted to be left alone or not. They'd both be staying at the same place, the saloon where the game was to be held, and Fargo figured he could keep an eye on Astor without too much trouble while they were there. The problem was that the poker game wasn't for two days, and Astor would be wandering around New Orleans during that time. Fargo had heard that New Orleans was a place where you didn't have to look for trouble. Trouble was happy to come looking for you.

Ashore, Fargo looked around. He didn't belong in the swirl of the mob, and he hated the hubbub. The smell of liquor was strong outside the grog shops, and it mingled with the odor of the fish and vegetables and flowers. Fargo preferred the smell of the pines on high lonesome mountains. He liked the space of the wide prairies, and wanted a high blue sky over his head.

Not knowing his way around the city, Fargo looked for a way to get to the place where he'd be staying. There were carriages for hire, and Fargo decided to take one. The driver was a wizened man with the stub of an unlit cigar sticking out of the corner of his mouth. He looked Fargo over and asked where he was going.

"A place called King Crawfish," Fargo said. "You know where that is?"

"I know, all right. But if you don't mind my sayin' so, you don't look like the kind of fella should be goin' to that place."

Fargo got in the carriage, settled back in the seat, and said, "Why not?"

"'Cause it's down on the end of Gallatin Street, that's why."

Fargo knew as much about the streets of New Orleans as a hog knew about geometry. He said, "What's wrong with Gallatin Street?"

"Worst street in Naw'lins. Now you're a big man, and I can tell by those clothes you're wearin' you're from rough country. I bet you've been in a tussle or two in your life, but that don't matter here. I don't care where you been or what you've done or how many men you might've killed, you ain't never seen nothin' like Gallatin Street."

"I'll have to see it now," Fargo said. "King Crawfish is where I'm staying. Don't worry about me, though."

"I ain't worryin' a bit," the driver said. "After all, I ain't the one stayin' on Gallatin Street."

13

What Fargo didn't know was that Gallatin Street was the end of the line in New Orleans. It was where the whores wound up when they were too sick or too old to earn a living elsewhere. It was home to criminals of all sorts: fences of stolen goods, killers, thieves, gamblers down on their luck, men who couldn't get work because they were so violent that they weren't tolerated in other parts of the city or the state, pickpockets, knife artists, confidence men, and shady operators of all kinds. A haven to people of all nations, Gallatin Street catered to their vices. If you wanted opium, it could be had. If your taste ran to perverse sex, it was available on a moment's notice. If you needed someone killed, there was a man who'd do the job for five dollars. There was plenty of gambling, too, but not much hope of finding an honest game.

Gallatin was a short street near the French Quarter, lined with buildings that stank of cheap liquor, unwashed bodies, and nearly every variety of filth known to man. A stranger wandering into the neighborhood was considered fair game and was lucky to get away with his life, much less with his money or his watch. If a man fell into the clutches of one of the grasping twilight women, his health was likely to undergo a sad and permanent decline.

Fargo's driver explained all this to him as they traveled away from the levee, through passages so narrow that Fargo could have reached out of the carriage and helped himself to fruit or oysters from one of the stands, or even a mug of beer from a bar.

"There are men down on Gallatin who'd just as soon slit your throat as tell you what day it is," the driver said. "Some of them'd do it just for fun or to pass the time. You take Bug-Eye John. I hear he killed his own brother in a fight over a bet they had."

"What about the King Crawfish?"

"Well, like I said, it's on the end of the street. The good end, you might say, if there is such a thing on Gallatin. Which there ain't, as you ought to've figgered out by now."

The little man drove in silence for a while. Then he said, "Name's Oscar. Oscar Robinson. I take it this is your first time in Naw'lins, bein' as you don't know about Gallatin."

Fargo told Oscar his name and said, "This is my first time here, all right. I heard about a big poker game at King Crawfish, so I thought I'd see what it was like."

Oscar clucked to his horse, which managed to avoid running over a boy hawking candy, and said, "My, my, my. A poker game at King Crawfish. Bound to be crooked as a dog's hind leg if you ask me. Never been a square game on Gallatin, not in the memory of a man livin'. I guess

Red Herman's turned honest. Maybe he's tryin' to change his ways."

"Red Herman?"

"That's the fella that owns King Crawfish. They call him that because of his hair. Looks so red, you'd swear somebody set it afire."

"But you haven't heard anything about this big game of his?"

"Nope. I generally steer clear of Gallatin and anybody associated with it. Might not've picked you up if I'd known where you was headin'. But since it's daylight, I don't mind all that much. Nobody on Gallatin wakes up till 'round about dark. In the daylight you might even be able to walk half a block before somebody pulls you into some alley and robs you or slits your gullet or steals your shoes."

Fargo thought about Red Herman and his big game while the carriage wound through the city streets. It was by far the most colorful place Fargo had ever been, and one of the noisiest. It seemed to him that there was music coming out of every third or fourth building they passed. He mentioned it to Oscar.

"Ever'body in Naw'lins loves music," Oscar said. "You might as well get used to it."

Fargo said he thought he could do that.

"We're just about there," Oscar said. "I hope you know what you're gettin' yourself into."

"I'm pretty sure I don't," Fargo said. "But that's nothing new."

Oscar stopped his horse in front of a two-story building that looked in somewhat better repair than any of those near it. Out front there was a painted sign that had a picture of a giant crawfish wearing a red crown. The words KING CRAWFISH were written above the creature's waving claws. Below it were the words GAMING, ROOMS, DRINKS.

"This is it," Oscar said.

Fargo got out of the carriage and paid him.

"Looks like they have everything a man could want," Fargo said, indicating the sign.

"Not me. Not on Gallatin Street. My, my, my. I liked all that when I was young. Not now. I like bein' alive too much."

"I like it, too," Fargo said.

"You watch yourself, now," Oscar told him, "or you won't be alive much longer. Don't go outside after dark, and if you have to go out, don't go wanderin' off down the street."

Fargo nodded, brushed away a mosquito, and took a whiff of the rancid air.

"Not exactly a rose garden, is it?" Oscar said.

He turned the carriage around and drove away while Fargo looked over his surroundings. Not the loveliest he'd ever seen, he thought, but not the worst, either. He'd slept in camps with men who hadn't bathed in months, seen starving men eat spoiled meat, stayed at trading posts where there were men so drunk they hadn't been able to stand for days. Gallatin Street couldn't be too much worse.

He walked inside the building, where the dim light didn't do much to hide the shabby furnishings. It looked as if it had been elegant once, but years of neglect had taken the shine off the wood, the nap off the cloth, the hope off the sallow face of the man behind the counter.

Fargo dropped his bag on the floor and asked if there was a room available.

"You here for the poker game?" the man asked.

He had sunken eyes and a sunken chest. Lank black hair hung low over his forehead.

"That's right," Fargo said. "I've been traveling with David Astor. He might be here already."

"Wouldn't know about that. You want a room, you got to sign the register and pay a day in advance."

Fargo scratched his name on the yellowed page of the book before him. He didn't see Astor's name there, but Daly and Shaw had signed in. The Winthrops had not, but then Fargo hadn't expected them to, not after hearing what Oscar had to say. Cam Winthrop might play in the card game, but he wouldn't be staying anywhere near a place like King Crawfish.

When Fargo had paid for a day in advance, the sallow man said, "Rooms are all here on the first floor. Yours is right over there, number twenty-three."

"My lucky number," Fargo said as the man laid a heavy key down on the counter with a clank.

"You might want to bet it on the wheel, then. The gambling's upstairs. Every game as straight as an arrow. Don't start till after dark, though."

"I noticed it was kind of quiet around here."

"Always is, daytimes. Livens up a good bit around nightfall."

"Any place I can get a meal around here?"

"We don't serve meals. You can go down the block to Marie's."

"Any place that's not on Gallatin?"

"Marie's is as good as you'll find anywhere in this town, even if it is on Gallatin. You give it a try." The man gave Fargo a contemptuous look. "Nothing to be scared of in the daytime."

The room wasn't quite as bad as he'd expected, but it wasn't anything to be proud of. The bed sagged, the paint was peeling off the wall, and the pitcher in the wash basin looked cracked. There was a spiderweb in one corner of the room. Fargo set his bag on the floor and went over to brush the web away. There was no spider. It had left long ago, maybe to find better lodgings.

When Fargo went back to his bag, he looked out the door and saw Astor standing at the counter. Everybody was there now, except Montgomery, and Fargo didn't figure him for a resident. He'd stay somewhere near the levee.

And then there was Amelia's statement. She'd said she might come by. Fargo wondered why. She hadn't seemed to him to be the kind of woman who'd want to spend any time in a place like King Crawfish. But then he'd known plenty of women who hadn't turned out to be what they seemed. Maybe Amelia was one.

He closed the door and opened the room's only window. It faced an alley foul with the smell of garbage and worse, but it was so stuffy and hot in the room that Fargo didn't think he could survive with the window closed. He wasn't sure he could survive with it open, either, and he didn't like the idea of an open window in a neighborhood like this one.

It was a little after noon, so Fargo decided he might as well give Marie's a try. The food couldn't be worse than some he'd eaten on the trail. It might even be better, and it should be interesting to have a look around Gallatin Street, even in the daylight.

The street didn't prove to be interesting at all. Most of the people Fargo saw were those going to Marie's, and they wanted to eat, not rob or kill some stranger. There was a man sleeping off a drunk in a doorway, or maybe he was dead. Fargo couldn't tell, and no one else paid him any attention. Flies buzzed around his half-open mouth.

A woman stepped out of an alley and asked Fargo if he wanted to have a little fun, but he could tell her heart wasn't in it. The sun shone on her ravaged face, making her look close to a hundred years old, and she ducked back in the shadows of the alley.

Marie's was a busy place, even if it was long before dark. The tables were crowded, and the waiters were bustling around carrying trays laden with food. The place smelled of fish and of spices that Fargo couldn't begin to identify.

He found a seat at a long table and read a menu scrawled in chalk on a board above the counter. He didn't know what half the stuff was, and he wasn't sure he was ready for crawfish pie or fried alligator tail. The fried oysters sounded good, though.

The man next to Fargo was slurping noisily from a soup bowl, and since he seemed to be enjoying it quite a bit, Fargo asked what he was having.

"Gumbo," the man said. "Best you can get in Naw'lins, and that's the truth."

The man had one eye, only a few teeth, and a long scar down the side of his face where someone had used a knife on him. He didn't look familiar with the truth, but Fargo thought he might as well try the gumbo.

"Get you some cornbread, too," the man said, so Fargo did.

When the gumbo came, it turned out to be surprisingly good, hot and spicy and a mixture of so many flavors that Fargo gave up trying to figure them out. He removed a couple of claws and set them on the table.

"Crabs," the man sitting beside him said.

Fargo nodded. He didn't care what was in the gumbo, as long as it didn't make him sick, and it tasted so good even getting sick might be worth it. The cornbread wasn't bad, either.

After he'd eaten, Fargo went back to the hotel. There was no one in the lobby except the sallow man at the desk, so Fargo went to his room and lay down on the sagging bed. The room was hot and steamy, but in only a few minutes, the Trailsman was asleep.

14

Fargo sat up. He was soaked in sweat, and his mouth tasted as if a crow had nested in it. There was a knock on the door, and he realized that an earlier knock must have awakened him. He got off the bed and stretched to take out the kinks the sagging mattress had given him.

There was another knock, louder, and David Astor's voice came to Fargo through the door.

"Come on, Fargo. I know you're there. Open the door."

Fargo didn't take orders too well. In fact, taking orders was one of his least favorite things. But he wanted to see Astor, so he stepped to the door and opened it.

"It's about time," Astor said. He pushed by Fargo and went into the room. "Shut the door."

Fargo didn't have any good reason not to close the door, so he did. Then he said, "I'm not your nursemaid anymore, Astor. So you can stop telling me what to do."

Astor didn't look a bit abashed. He said, "Sorry. I tend to get impatient now and then."

There was one chair in the room, but both men stood. Astor looked out the window.

"Not much of a view," he said. "But the smell makes up for it."

Fargo had to grin at that. He said, "Maybe I'll get used to it. Did you know what kind of place this was?"

"Yes. I've been to New Orleans before, so I'd heard

about this part of town. I'd never been here, but I knew more or less what to expect."

"I didn't. So what I want to know is about this poker game. I'm not much of a gambler, but I'd say this isn't the kind of place for a really big game."

"It wouldn't be, usually. It's Red Herman's idea. He wants to turn this place into a real gambling palace."

"He has a long way to go."

"I know that, but he's managed to get a lot of card players here, and most of them have plenty of money."

"Not you, though."

"Not me." Astor looked at the floor. "That's why I'm here."

"I don't have enough money to stake you if that's what you're after."

"That's not it. I was wondering if you might talk to Cam Winthrop. He has plenty of money. If he'd let me borrow a little, I could get in the game. I won a little last night, but not enough."

"I don't know Winthrop that well," Fargo said.

"You know Ida, though. You talked to her about me before, and you could do it again."

Fargo said, "You know her better than I do."

"She doesn't care anything about me. I tried to talk to her this morning, and she brushed me off. She's pretending to be awfully devoted to Cam today, but I think she and Montgomery have something cooked up. It's all your fault, too."

Fargo didn't bother to say that he'd only been trying to save Astor's neck. If Ida Winthrop had made some kind of arrangement with Montgomery, that was between the two of them, and Fargo hadn't had a thing to do with it.

"I don't know where she's staying," Fargo said. "And I don't ask women for money."

"I can tell you where she's staying. And you wouldn't be asking her for money, really. I would, or you'd be asking for me, and it wouldn't be the same thing. I need the money, Fargo. I have to get into this game to win enough money to keep on going. Chloe would want you to do this."

Fargo didn't know whether the part about Chloe was true or not, but he said he'd think it over.

"You don't care much for me, do you?"

74

"Let's just say you're a little different from what I'd been led to believe."

"Look, Fargo. I've done a few things wrong in my life. I know that. But I didn't ever kill anybody, if that's what you're thinking."

"It's not that," Fargo said.

"You've probably been listening to people who don't much like me. Sure, Daly and Shaw seem friendly, but they don't really care for me. I don't know why."

"I do," Fargo said.

"All right, maybe I do, too. But Shaw was cheating in that game. Everybody knew it. It's just that I was the only one with the guts to say so."

"We've talked about this before. He's not the only one you accused."

"Look, if people are taking my money and I know they're running a crooked game, I have an obligation to tell them so."

Fargo didn't want to get into an another argument about it.

"Maybe so," he said.

"And Daly. His wife forced herself on me. Women like me. I can't help it. Now are you going to talk to Ida or not?"

"If I see her, I'll mention it to her."

"You're afraid of Montgomery, aren't you?" Astor said. "That must be it. Otherwise you wouldn't mind doing this for me."

Fargo just looked at him.

"He called me in for what he called 'a little talk' this morning," Astor continued. "That's why I was late getting off the boat. You didn't get off until I did, so I guess he must have gotten you in his cabin, too."

"I'm not afraid of Montgomery."

"I don't blame you if you are. Anyone with any sense would be. There was something . . . but never mind that. It wouldn't matter to you. Something else would, though. He told me that I'd have to answer to him if I saw Ida again. Did he say the same thing to you?"

Fargo's opinion of Astor went down nearly every time they met lately. The gambler wasn't just a womanizer and accuser. He was also a coward. It was one thing to challenge men in front of a group who would do their best to prevent a fight. Anyone could do that. It was another thing to stand up to someone in private, and apparently Astor couldn't do that.

Fargo was tired of his whining. He said, "I'll talk to her. If I can find her. I'm not going to look very hard."

"You won't have to. She's at the St. James Hotel, not far from a restaurant called Antoine's. Everyone in town knows where Antoine's is. You could probably catch her in her room this afternoon if you went over."

"I have a feeling her husband wouldn't be too happy if I did that," Fargo said, thinking that Montgomery wouldn't be too happy about it, either, if he found out. Not that Fargo cared.

"He's probably drunk or playing cards. If you go right now, she'll be alone. You have to do this, Fargo. It's my only chance. Please."

Fargo didn't like men who begged. Another mark against Astor.

"All right," Fargo said. "I'll go talk to her."

"Thanks, Fargo. You won't regret this."

Fargo wasn't so sure. In fact, he was already regretting it.

The St. James was in considerably better condition than King Crawfish. The lobby was hung with velvet, and the gilt shone. The desk clerk was alert and dressed better than anybody Fargo had met in New Orleans.

"I'll send word up to the room that you're here," he told Fargo when the Trailsman asked to see Mrs. Winthrop.

Fargo had decided on the direct approach, and it worked. He sat in a wing chair and waited. In only a short time, a smartly dressed bellman walked up to him and said, "Follow me, sir."

"Where are we going?" Fargo wanted to know.

"To the Winthrops' room, sir. Mrs. Winthrop wants to see you."

"What about Mr. Winthrop?"

"I didn't inquire, sir."

The bellman must have been on the job a long time, as there was only the slightest insinuation in the man's tone. Fargo ignored it. He rose out of the chair and said, "All right. Let's go."

Ida Winthrop was waiting. She was loosely wrapped in a gown that to Fargo looked to be made of gauze and feathers. There was plenty of Ida showing through, and the revealing garment made her seem more immodest than if she'd been completely naked.

"It's nice to see you again, Fargo," she said.

"You seemed glad enough to leave me last night," Fargo said.

"Oh, that was simply a little misunderstanding." Ida lifted a hand to fan her face, and the motion redistributed the gauze and feathers. It was plain that she was wearing nothing else and that she was deliberately displaying herself for Fargo.

"Is it hot in here?" she asked. "Or is it just me?"

Fargo was getting plenty warm himself as he looked at the libidinous Mrs. Winthrop. Her trim ankles and long slim legs were fully exposed. Her thighs were tight and firm.

"Cat got your tongue?" Ida asked after several seconds of silence.

"No," Fargo said, trying to keep his voice level. "I'm still wondering about last night."

"Just put it out of your mind. I'm sorry it happened." She paused to fan her face again. "Not all of it, of course. Just the ending."

"I guess you didn't hear anything from that letter writer, then."

"No, I didn't. You were right. I was silly to worry about it. It was just someone hoping to scare David, and it didn't work."

"I think David was plenty scared," Fargo said. "But not about that."

"It doesn't matter. You were much more fun than David could ever be."

Fargo thought it was time to change the subject. He looked around the room and said, "Where's your husband?"

"Cameron." She said the name as she would have said the name of a pet dog that was in disfavor. "He's out gambling. Must stay sharp for the big game, you know. He won't be back for quite a while. Are you sure you're not hot, Fargo? This weather is almost more than I can bear."

Ida wriggled a little, and even more of her creamy skin was exposed. Fargo could see the hard dark tips of her breasts peeking at him from among the feathers, and he felt himself responding.

"I came here to ask you for something," he said.

"Well, well. If you ask nicely, I just might give it to you."

"It's not what you're thinking."

Ida slid a hand down among the feathers where the gown ended. Her fingers disappeared into the feathers in the region where Fargo had just glimpsed some wiry copper hairs.

"David Astor needs five hundred dollars."

"That's a lot of money. But I might be able to get it from Cameron. He likes to give me money. You'd owe me a favor, though, Fargo."

Fargo didn't want her to think he owed her a thing.

"Not me," he said. "Astor."

Ida sat up straighter in the chair and adjusted her feathery garment. It still hid very few of her charms.

"That's not nearly as much fun. I'd much rather it be you."

Fargo didn't care what she wanted. He wasn't going to give in, even if Astor didn't get the money. He didn't care that much about Astor, either.

"It's not going to be me," he said.

Ida pouted for a second, then smiled and said, "Very well, then. Are you sure you don't want anything else?"

"Wanting doesn't have anything to do with it," Fargo said.

Ida took a pointed glance at the growing bulge in Fargo's pants.

"I can see you're telling the truth about that much. You're a complicated man, Fargo."

"No, just somebody who has trouble figuring out a woman like you. Last night you didn't want to have any more to do with me. Today, well, today's different."

"I was angry last night. I wanted a favor, and I thought you were the man to do it. But you weren't. That's all there is to it."

"But you're willing to do a favor for me today," Fargo said.

"Not for you," she reminded him. "For David."

"Right. For David. I know he'll appreciate it."

"He'll have the money tomorrow," Ida said, shrugging her shoulders in and shifting far enough forward in her seat to put her most ample charms on display. "Are you really sure I can't convince you to enjoy something while you're here?"

"Yes," Fargo said. He swallowed hard. "I'm sure."

Ida's eyes closed languidly, and a smile played around the corners of her mouth.

"Then good-bye, Fargo," she said.

When he went out the door he could hear her sighs at his back.

Astor was elated when Fargo gave him the news.

"When will I get the money?" he asked.

Fargo said that Ida had promised it tomorrow.

"Damn. Well, it doesn't matter as long as I'm getting it. I'm sure she'll send it over. It's just a drop in the bucket to a man like Winthrop. He won't even miss it."

Fargo didn't know what kind of man wouldn't miss five hundred dollars, but he didn't say that. Instead, he said, "I hope you're going to stay out of trouble from now on."

"Don't start that again," Astor said. "I can take care of myself. I don't need you watching me all the time."

"You've got me, though," Fargo told him. "I got you the money, and now you're going to return the favor. I'm going to stick to you and get you through this because I promised your sister. After that, I don't give a damn what you do."

Astor looked as if he were about to tell Fargo to go to hell, but if that was so, he changed his mind. He said, "All right. If that's the way you want it. I'm going to my room now. Are you coming with me?"

"I don't want to get that close. Just let me know if you plan to go out. I hear it's not a good idea to do that after dark."

Astor shrugged. "A man has to eat."

"That's true. Knock on the door before you leave and I'll go with you."

"Daly and Shaw might want to come along."

"That's all right with me," Fargo said, though he wasn't much fonder of those two than he was of David.

"We'll show you a good time," David said.

"I don't doubt that," Fargo told him.

15

Fargo and Astor stood outside the King Crawfish, breathing the thick evening air. Mosquitoes buzzed and hummed in front of their faces. There was a mass of heavy black clouds hanging back in the western sky, and Fargo heard the low rumble of distant thunder. Flickers of lightning brightened the sky for a brief moment before fading.

Fargo had always associated rain with cooler weather, but it didn't work that way in New Orleans. The muggy heat clung to him like the memory of a bad dream.

"How do people live in this town?" he said. "I don't see how they can ever get used to the heat."

"They don't get used to it," Astor said. "They just learn to live with it."

"What happened to Daly and Shaw?" Fargo asked. "I thought you said they'd be coming with us."

"Daly wanted to play four-ball billiards. He can make some money if the other players don't know him. Shaw went along to place some side bets."

"Daly's that good?"

"He's one of the best. That's why he likes to play in a new town where he's not known. Nobody who knows how good he is will play against him. But as good as he is at billiards, he likes playing cards better."

It was early evening, but with the dark clouds obscuring most of the sky, it felt like night. Gallatin Street was coming alive.

Most of the people that Fargo saw as they walked past the hotel seemed in a hurry, as if there was too much light there on that end of the street and they preferred the darkness farther on. They averted their faces as they passed, not wanting anyone to get a good look at them. Many were poorly dressed, some even in rags, but now and then someone in nice clothing would wander by. Those people were in no hurry, and they weren't hiding. They glanced about them with avid curiosity, taking everything in, getting a good look at the lowlife as they began their evening's adventure. Fargo figured that some of them would be getting a lot more adventure than they really wanted, and he guessed that one or two might not be leaving Gallatin Street when morning came.

"We might as well go on and find something to eat," Astor said. "Daly and Shaw won't be back any time soon."

"We could go to that place you told me about," Fargo said. "Antoine's."

"Too expensive. I don't have that money from Ida yet. Besides, Marie's is just as good."

Fargo didn't argue. He'd enjoyed the gumbo, and he wouldn't mind trying something else there. New Orleans might have a hellish climate, but so far the food had been good.

The street was dark, but Fargo could see in to some of the places they passed. In one of them, women danced in gowns that covered less than the feathery frock Ida Winthrop had worn earlier, and the men watching the women dance smiled avidly as they drank their watered whiskey.

A little farther on, a bouncer was dragging an unconscious man through a doorway. It was such a common sight that hardly anyone noticed except Fargo. The bouncer tossed the man into one of the many side alleys, and before Fargo had gone two more steps, three men from the street had rushed into the alley to strip the unconscious man of whatever the bouncer had left him.

Fargo smelled the stench of unwashed bodies, raw liquor, the muck of the alleys, and decades of decay. It was enough to make a man lose his appetite.

Astor must have felt the same way.

"This is quite a place," he said, a little worriedly.

"I hear that you can pretty much do whatever you can get away with here," Fargo said, and before the words were out of his mouth he felt a delicate touch, so light that most men wouldn't have noticed it at all. But Fargo was fully alert, his senses functioning as they would if he were in hostile Indian territory.

He reached down, grabbed a thin wrist, and dragged a small figure out of the shadows.

"Hello, Fargo," Duma said, smiling up at him.

"You know this ragamuffin?" Astor said.

"We've met," Fargo said. "What are you doing here, Duma?"

"Earning a living," said a voice from the darkness nearby, and Rastin stepped out so Fargo could see him.

"This is no place for a girl," Fargo told the Gypsy. "Or anybody else."

"You are here," Rastin pointed out. "And your friend."

"We have a good reason to be."

"So do we. A Gypsy is at home anywhere, and it is not easy to find jobs in a new city. So we come to places like this, where money can be had for the taking."

"If you don't get caught."

Rastin laughed. "Duma would not have been caught had she not recognized you. She is much too clever for that. She was not trying to take your money. She wanted only to greet you again."

"This place is too dangerous for you, Duma," Fargo said.

The girl echoed Rastin's laugh. "No place is too dangerous for us. There are many of us, and we all look out for one another."

From somewhere down an alley, a scream echoed through the hubbub of the street. Then it was cut off abruptly. No one paid any attention except Fargo and Rastin, who both looked in that direction.

"There are more dangerous things here than on any steamboat," Fargo said, turning back to face Rastin.

"You should know about danger, Fargo," Rastin said. "You found plenty of it. Come, Duma. It is time for us to look for other, richer men."

"Good-bye," Duma said, and she and Rastin faded into the shadows so quietly and swiftly it was hard to believe they'd ever been there. Fargo hoped that they wouldn't find Gallatin Street more dangerous than they thought it was.

"You have some odd friends, Fargo," Astor said.

"I could say the same for you. At least I trust those two. I can't say the same for Daly and Shaw."

"They don't mean anything by their joking," Astor said. "Even if they do have reason to dislike me, they've never tried to hurt me."

Fargo wasn't as sure of that as Astor seemed to be. He said, "Not that you know about."

Astor grinned crookedly. "You're too cynical. You need to put more trust in people."

There were few enough people that Fargo trusted, and he didn't intend to add Daly and Shaw to the list. Or Astor, for that matter.

"Come on," he said. "I'm getting hungry." And it was true, in spite of the smell.

Astor nodded, and they made their way through the motley crowd. More people appeared every minute it seemed, and Fargo thought that Oscar Robinson had surely been right. There wasn't a one of them that wouldn't slit your throat for a dollar or just to see you fall and die.

Dark clouds were overhead now, and thunder was loud enough to drown out some of the noise of the street. The lightning illuminated the undersides of the clouds and deepened the shadows around the buildings. Fargo caught a glimpse of someone off to one side, someone he thought he recognized, but the darkness returned and the person disappeared. Fargo shrugged it off, thinking that he couldn't have been right.

Just before Fargo and Astor reached Marie's, the rain started to fall. It was as if the sky had opened up and dumped the Gulf of Mexico on them, huge drops of water falling thick as a curtain. Fargo was glad to get out of it before he got soaked. It would have been almost as bad as being in the river again.

The atmosphere in Marie's was different from earlier in the day. It was even louder, there were more customers, and while the air still held the smell of fish and spices, it was now soupy with steam, as if the heat from outside had been driven inside by the rain.

Astor said, "Have you ever tried jambalaya?"

Fargo said that he'd tried the gumbo, but that was all.

"If you liked that, you'll love the jambalaya," Astor said, so that was what they ordered.

It turned out to be a concoction of shrimp, oysters, and sausage served on rice with a spicy tomato sauce. Fargo wasn't sure it was any better than the gumbo, but it was certainly good enough.

"You can eat more good food in this town than any-where in the country," Astor said when they had finished. "If people here don't know anything else, they know how to cook, and they know how to eat."

By the time they left Marie's the rain had stopped, but a thick mist hung in the air, and steam seemed to rise from the muddy street. If anything, it was hotter outside than before the rain had fallen. Fargo took off his hat and wiped sweat from his forehead. While he had his hat off, he used it to fan away the mosquitoes. They hadn't been at all dis-couraged by the downpour. They retreated briefly when Fargo fanned at them, but by the time his hat was back on his head, they were at him again. Fargo made himself a promise that he wouldn't be coming back to New Orleans any time soon, no matter how good the food was.

The street was more crowded than it had been earlier. People pushed by, and Fargo heard someone groaning in an alley. Probably someone else a bouncer had thrown there, or maybe some hapless gent who thought he could survive a night on Gallatin Street and tell his friends about it the next day.

"You think we could find a card game around here?" Astor said.

"I don't care if we can," Fargo told him. "We're going back to the hotel. You can find a game there if you want one. But I didn't think you were crazy enough to believe you could build a stake by gambling."

"You're right," Astor said. "I'm not. But thanks for re-minding me. I'll just wait until I get my hands on Win-throp's money."

They started back toward the King Crawfish, and once again Fargo glimpsed someone out of the corner of his eye. This time he was sure they were being followed. He was about to mention it to Astor when an arm snaked out of the alley they had just passed and hooked the stalker around the neck. The arm and the stalker both vanished into the gloom.

Fargo decided a number of things at once.

The groans in the alley had been merely a cover-up to disguise the fact that someone was lying in wait.

Whoever was in there had been waiting for the stalker. And the stalker was undoubtedly Amelia.

16

By the time Amelia had screamed once, Fargo was at the entrance to the alley, leaving Astor behind to fend for himself. That might be a mistake, but Fargo couldn't help it. Amelia was in more immediate danger than the gambler. Fargo couldn't let her be hurt, and he wanted to find out why she was following him.

At the end of the alley, a dark figure pulled the struggling Amelia along. She had been wearing a hood, but it had fallen away, and Fargo could see her blond hair as her head shook from side to side. The Trailsman plunged into the alley, his boots sinking into soft mud. Lifting his foot took an extra effort, not only because his boots were becoming heavier but because the mud tried to hold him down. Each time he took a step there was a sucking sound as he pulled away from the viscous, clinging earth. He slogged down the alley at half speed.

Even at that, he was gaining on Amelia and her attacker. She was digging in her heels and holding him back. Fargo couldn't make out the man's face, and not just because of the darkness. He was wearing a hood and something that covered his face. Fargo had torn the mask off his attacker when he'd fallen over the side of *The Wanderer*, but if this was the same person, it must have been replaced.

The alley appeared to end at the back of a building, but that was misleading. It joined another alley that ran along behind the buildings on Gallatin Street. The masked figure dragged Amelia to the right and disappeared.

Fargo plodded on. The alley was foul with the smell of human waste, garbage, and decay. Every odor reeked up at him when he pulled a boot from the mud. He came to the turn, and saw two murky figures on the left. A man was having sex with a woman who was braced against a wall as he entered her from the rear. Her dress was thrown up over her back, and neither of them seemed in the least bothered by Fargo's sudden appearance. He supposed they hadn't been bothered when Amelia and her assailant had passed, either. Certainly they'd made no attempt to stop them. He couldn't blame them. They were too occupied with their own diversions to care much about anyone else.

Fargo turned to the right. There was more light at that end of the alley, and Fargo could see that Amelia was still struggling. But then he heard Amelia's scream cut off abruptly as if the arm around her neck had finally throttled her.

The man dragged her suddenly limp body across a small square of light thrown by a lamp-lit window. The hooded man was dragging her along more easily now. But Fargo was getting closer, and he might have caught up to them if he hadn't stumbled and gone sprawling forward into the mire, sliding along for a couple of feet before coming to a stop with his face in the filth.

He stood up and slung mud from his eyes, nose, and mouth, but Amelia and the man who had snatched her were gone. Fargo heard a moan behind him and realized he'd stepped on the out-flung arm of a man lying there, whether drunk or hurt the Trailsman didn't know, and it didn't matter. His interest was elsewhere.

"This way, Fargo," someone said. "They are not far."

"Rastin, you're beginning to bother me," Fargo said, recognizing the voice. "You pop up all the time, like some kind of ghost."

"Do not forget that I am responsible for you. But this time, I was not watching over you. Your friends interrupted me as I was relieving a man of his valuables."

"They're not my friends. Well, one of them isn't. The woman needs help."

"I suppose I can take the rest of the man's valuables

later, if someone else does not come along and do it. We had better go or you will be too late to help the woman."

Fargo followed the Gypsy down the alley to the back of a dark building.

"They went inside," Rastin said. "The man seemed to know where he was going."

"Where's Duma?" Fargo asked.

"She is safe. You do not have to worry about Duma. We take care of our own. Do you know who you are chasing?"

"I know one of them," Fargo said. "And I want to get to know the other one."

He stepped onto a small wooden porch, and put his hand on the door latch. The door swung inward at his touch. Fargo drew his Colt.

"I feel that I should advise against you entering," Rastin said. "It would not be good for my reputation if you were to be killed."

"I won't worry about Duma if you'll quit worrying about me."

"That sounds almost reasonable. Unfortunately, it is not. You are my responsibility, whether I like it or not. And now, I confess, I do not like it."

"Good. Go back and finish with that fella you knocked in the mud, and leave this to me."

"He fell," Rastin said. "I hardly touched him."

Fargo didn't dignify that comment with a response. He entered the building, leaving the Gypsy standing in the alley.

It was darker than the inside of a hibernating bear in a mountain cave. Fargo stood still for a while, hoping that his eyes would become accustomed to the deep gloom. He soon was able to make out a few shapes that resembled covered furniture. There was no sign of Amelia or her abductor.

The thought entered Fargo's mind that he had been led into an elaborate trap. What if the hooded man had lured him here to kill him? He'd tried to do that on the boat, and failed. There was nothing to stop him from trying again.

There was also nothing to stop him from luring Fargo away from David Astor while someone else killed the gambler, but Fargo didn't think that was going to happen. Whoever was after David wanted him to suffer, not die.

Fargo felt a touch on his shoulder, and it was all he could do not to jump.

"I do not think you should go farther," Rastin said.

Fargo was getting really tired of the Gypsy, even though his intentions seemed good. He said, "Look, if you want to do me a favor, go out to the street and look for David Astor. Do you know who he is?"

"He was on the boat, a gambler, not a well-bred man."

"That's him, all right. I'm sort of responsible for him the way you're responsible for me, but I have to find out why that woman was dragged in here and I can't watch out for him. You could do that for me."

"Very well, but if you die here, I will feel terrible for weeks. And I may lose my position with my people."

"Just go," Fargo said, and Rastin faded out the door, leaving Fargo in the darkened room.

The Trailsman still could see very little, so he stood still and listened. There was no sound of breathing, no scrape of a boot on the floor, no rustle of clothing. Which meant that there was no one else in the room with him. No one could be so quiet that Fargo couldn't hear him in an enclosed space. Either the hooded man had left, or had never been there at all. Of course, there could be a staircase leading to another floor, and the man could have gone there, taking Amelia with him.

Fargo felt his way around the walls until he located the stairway. He stopped at its foot and listened again. He thought he heard something, but it could have been no more than a rat running across the floorboards.

If it was a rat, Fargo thought, it was a human rat. The Trailsman started up the stairs, walking as close to the wall as he could in the hope he'd avoid a creaking board. He was successful, and reached the second-floor landing without making a sound. He tried to see where he was and what was around him. It was hopeless. If anything, this floor was darker than the first. Fargo was reduced to feeling his way along the hall.

He figured the place was an old hotel, long abandoned. There was a musty smell about it, and he doubted anyone had stayed there in a long time, other than people seeking refuge from Gallatin Street. He could smell their leavings over the scent of must and decay, but none of them were in there now. The old building was hot, muggy, and stuffy. Fargo didn't blame even the vagrants for avoiding it.

There were doors on both sides of the hallway, and Fargo didn't know where his quarry could be hiding. Each time he came to an open door, he looked into the room beyond it. He pointed his pistol inside as well, but saw nothing to shoot at in the black shadows. And he heard nothing until there was a light step behind him and something hard, like the end of a cane, struck him between the shoulder blades.

Fargo felt a sharp pain, as if he'd been stabbed. He fell forward into a somersault, and when he came up he whirled around, his finger tightening on the Colt's trigger.

He didn't pull it because a piece of solid wood smacked him on the side of the head. The blow sounded like two blocks of wood coming together, and it knocked him against the wall. It was still very dark in the hallway but now there were stars and little points of light dancing along it. Oddly enough, they did nothing to illuminate the darkness. Fargo realized that he'd dropped the pistol and that he had no idea where it was. His head throbbed like the tight skin of an Indian drum.

The next blow hit him on the left shoulder. That was getting to be a habit, and he didn't like it at all. As on the previous night, his arm was virtually paralyzed.

Fargo flattened himself to the floor, dust filling his mouth and nose, and he heard a ringing sound as the club hit the wall over his head and bounced back.

The Trailsman slithered forward like a snake. He turned onto his side and reached out, grabbing the feet of the man with the bludgeon. He pulled hard, and the man's legs flew out from under him, flipping him backward. His head hit the floor, and the club rattled against the wall.

Rolling over the man, Fargo reached for the club with his good arm, but the man threw him aside.

Fargo felt emptiness behind him and rolled into an open room, but he didn't try to close the door. He wanted the man to come in after him, but he'd want it more if he could find something to fight back with. He stood up, moved around behind the door, and waited.

When he heard a footstep, he slammed the door as hard as he could, following its arc with his right shoulder shoving against it.

It smacked into the man, causing him to cry out and drop his retrieved stick. The man stumbled backward. Fargo snatched the door open and rushed out. The man had staggered against a closed door across the hall, and Fargo crashed into him.

The door shattered into splinters, and Fargo and the man fell into the empty room. Dust flew up from the floor, nearly choking Fargo, but he got atop the man, locking his legs tightly to his sides and locking his hands around his throat.

The man pitched and bucked like an unbroken horse, but Fargo held on, squeezing as hard as he could, considering that he didn't have much of a grip with his left hand.

After a long while, or maybe a short one, Fargo couldn't tell, the man stopped struggling and lay still. The blood beat in Fargo's temples, and a knot was rising on one side of his head. His breath rasped in his throat. He wanted to keep right on squeezing the man's throat until there was no question that he'd never move again, but the Trailsman made his fingers open. Then he sat astride the man and breathed raggedly until he was feeling a little less in a killing mood. He wiped sweat from his forehead and stood up.

Fargo didn't think the unconscious man would be going anywhere, not for a good while, so he located his pistol and went to look for Amelia. He hadn't gotten far before he stepped on the man's club. It turned under his foot, and he would have fallen if he hadn't been near the wall. He put out an arm to catch himself, and when steady, he reached down, picked up the club, and turned it in his hands. It wasn't a cane, though it was very much like one. Fargo tossed it aside and entered the next room.

He felt his way around, and for a while he thought the room was empty. Then his foot encountered a soft and yielding form. He knelt down and raised Amelia up. She was unconscious, but her breathing was slow and regular.

Fargo left her where she was and returned to the other room. He knew who was lying on the floor now, and he wanted to get both him and Amelia out of there. He ripped off the man's face covering and tore it into strips, binding his hands behind his back. It wasn't easy in the darkness, but Fargo managed to get it done.

Just as he finished, he heard a noise.

Leaving the room, he saw a light moving up the stairs.

17

David Astor stood uncertainly at the top of the stairway, the lantern light behind him bouncing shadows off the wall. Someone gave Astor him a little push, and he stumbled forward. Fargo wasn't surprised to see Rastin in back of the gambler, holding a lantern.

"Fargo?" Astor said. "Is that you?"

"It's me."

"Why did you run away like that and then have this ruffian accost me? I thought he was going to drag me into the alley and kill me."

"A woman was following us," Fargo said. "And then she was grabbed. I wanted to find out what was going on."

"Well, you didn't have to leave me like that. I could have been murdered."

"Rastin wouldn't let that happen. He's a friend of mine."

"Your friends get odder and odder."

Fargo said, "Bring that lantern on down here, Rastin. You come, too, Astor."

Rastin stepped around Astor to where Fargo stood. Astor followed him, and Fargo led them into the room. While they watched, Fargo turned over the body on the floor.

"Daly," Astor said. "What's he doing here?"

"That's what I'd like to know," Fargo said. "He tried to kill me last night on the boat, and I'm sure he's the one who threatened to tell Cam Winthrop about you and Ida."

Astor kicked the unconscious man in the side. Daly moved an inch or two, but didn't come to.

"The son of a bitch," Astor said. "He's the one who's been killing the men who won money from me."

"I don't think so," Fargo said.

Astor kicked Daly again. "He has to be. It's not my fault his wife liked me. Now he's trying to get even."

Rastin watched stoically. Fargo took hold of Astor's arm and pulled him back.

"I don't care what he's done," Fargo said. "You don't kick a man when he's unconscious and tied up. Besides, he's not the only one who was following us tonight. There's a woman in the next room."

Fargo took the lantern from Rastin and left. The two men followed him into the room where Amelia lay. She was sitting up now, rubbing her neck. Looking up at Fargo, she said, "What happened?"

"Somebody grabbed you and brought you here."

She nodded. "I remember. Where is he?"

"He's in the next room. Why were you following us?"

Amelia looked down at the floor.

"I wasn't following anyone."

"Yes, you were," Fargo said.

Now that he thought of it, Fargo recalled that she had seemed awfully interested in Astor. Both times she had been with Fargo, she had asked about the gambler.

"Do you know her?" he asked Astor.

"She's the waitress from the boat," Astor said. "The one who remembered your lucky number."

"She's more than that. I think she knows you."

"She's just some slut. I never saw her before."

That appeared to be too much for Amelia. She stood up, with a little help from Fargo. Then, shrugging off Fargo's assistance, she slapped Astor's face.

The gambler was surprised and took a step backward. But he recovered quickly and drew back his arm as if to strike her back.

Rastin stepped between them.

"A man might kick another who is unable to defend himself and still retain his honor. But no man strikes a woman and does so."

"Who the hell are you to tell me what to do?" Astor said.

"I am Rastin," the Gypsy said, as if that was enough.

Astor glared at him but did nothing more. Fargo didn't blame him. Having had a little taste of Rastin's fists, the

Trailsman knew what Astor could have expected had he pushed things.

Amelia stepped up beside Rastin and said to Astor, "You can call me whatever names you want, but I'll never be as low as you are."

"I don't know you," Astor said. "Why are you saying things like that?"

"You knew my brother," Amelia said. "Thomas Lightsey."

Astor looked at her blankly. It was plain that he didn't know what she was talking about.

"He was just a boy from a little town in Missouri," Amelia said. "But he liked to play cards. He thought he could make a living at it and spend his life on the river in the paddle-wheelers like you and your friends."

"There's nothing wrong with that," Astor said.

"He wasn't as good as he thought. Not nearly as good. You ruined him."

"Then I did him a favor. If a man can't gamble, he shouldn't try to make a living at it."

"You didn't do him any favors." Amelia's face was flushed with anger. "After you took everything he had, he killed himself. It was your fault, and I hope you pay for it."

Astor seemed surprised at her vehemence.

"You can't blame me for what your brother did to himself. He should have found a way to get more money."

"Maybe he didn't know any women to get it from," Fargo said.

"What's that supposed to mean?"

"Nothing," Fargo said.

"I think Daly and this woman were working together," Astor said. "They've been killing people and putting the blame on me because they think I've wronged them. We have to take them to the police."

"We're not taking them to the police," Fargo said.

"What? Why not?"

"Because I'm not sure what they've done. I'd like to find out."

"You said Daly tried to kill you, and you can see that she hates me. What more do you need to know about them?"

"Plenty," Fargo said. He handed the lantern back to Rastin. "I'm going to get Daly and then we'll get out of here."

"If you're not going to the police, where are you taking them?" Astor said.

"To the King Crawfish," Fargo told him.

Out on Gallatin Street nobody noticed that Fargo was walking along with a bound man tossed over his shoulder. Or maybe it was just that people on Gallatin Street preferred to mind their own business. Amelia walked in front of them, and Astor walked just behind. The gambler was twirling Daly's billiard cue between his fingers in a way that aggravated Fargo, but the Trailsman didn't comment on it. Rastin faded back into the alley, perhaps to finish what he'd begun before Fargo had interrupted him.

Even at the King Crawfish, Fargo's entrance didn't cause much of a stir. It was a semi-respectable hotel, but it was located on Gallatin Street, after all. Its clientele had seen more than one man brought in unconscious, Fargo figured. He crossed the lobby and entered his room, tossing Daly on the sagging bed. The gambler groaned and twisted around.

"He's coming to," Astor said, tapping the end of the cue on the floor. "Ask him about those men he's killed."

Fargo didn't ask Daly anything. He told Astor to close the door and turned to Amelia.

"Why did Daly snatch you?" he asked.

"I don't know. I didn't know who it was until I saw him on the floor of that place where he took me. I saw him on the boat, but I never spoke to him."

"She's lying," Astor said. "They're in this together, framing me for murders I didn't do."

It was stifling in the room. The open window didn't help a thing. It just let in more sultry air. Fargo could feel the sweat running down his legs inside his pants.

"I didn't ask what you thought," Fargo told Astor.

"I'm the one they're trying to ruin," Astor said. "I have a right to find out why they're doing it."

"You played around with Daly's wife. You won all the money Amelia's brother had, and then he killed himself."

"But that's no reason for them to try to ruin me," Astor protested.

Fargo decided that Astor was one of those people who would always believe that their own actions were perfectly

94

understandable and acceptable, whereas the things others did were always unreasonable and unjustifiable.

"The truth is," Fargo said, "I don't think they were trying to ruin you. But why don't we ask your friend Daly?"

Daly was moaning and trying to sit up. He didn't seem to know just where he was or what had happened to him.

"You've been mighty busy the last couple of nights," Fargo said, helping Daly sit on the edge of the bed. "You want to tell us what you've been up to?"

Daly tried to speak, but his voice came out as a dry croak. Fargo had squeezed his throat a little too hard.

"Go get him something to drink," Fargo told Astor.

Astor looked for just a second as if he might not do it, but Fargo kept his eyes on him, and the gambler left the room.

"What about you?" Fargo asked Amelia. "What were you doing out there tonight?"

"I was just following Astor."

"You must have had something else in mind."

Amelia smiled. "I did. It wasn't much of a plan, but I was thinking that if I could distract you, Astor might wander off and get himself in trouble. Maybe even get himself killed. That could happen on Gallatin Street."

"How were you planning to distract me?"

"I don't know. You treated me nice, and I thought you liked me. Maybe you would have been interested in sporting me around."

"That's why you came to my room the other night? To distract me?"

"Well, I wanted to find out more about Astor if I could. And there was another reason."

"What was it?"

Amelia looked down at the floor and blushed.

"You know," she said.

Fargo said that he guessed he did, and at that moment Astor came back into the room with a glass of whiskey.

Fargo took the glass and was about to hand it to Daly when he remembered what had happened to Hollister.

"You take a little sip," he told Astor, handing the glass back.

"Why?"

"Just to make me feel better," Fargo said.

Astor looked at him quizzically, then took a small swallow.

"It's pretty raw," he said, "but it's the best they have around here."

"It'll do," Fargo said.

He took the glass and gave it to Daly, who swallowed most of the whiskey and coughed violently.

"Jesus!" he croaked. "My throat!"

"Somebody choked you," Fargo said. "Maybe you remember why."

Daly drank the rest of the whiskey. This time he didn't cough as much.

Fargo sleeved sweat from his forehead. He said, "Maybe you don't remember. So I'll tell you. Last night you followed me out onto the deck of the boat and then tried to kill me. Tonight you were following me again."

"I wasn't intending to hurt you," Daly said, his voice straining. "And I wasn't following you."

"Who were you following, then?"

Daly looked up. "Astor."

"I told you," Astor said. "He was out to get me. I'm going for the police."

Fargo suspected those words had never been spoken inside the King Crawfish before that night. He said, "No. Let's hear what he has to say. Daly, why were you following Astor? And why attack me and Amelia?"

"It was like this," Daly said, his voice growing a bit stronger. "I was after Astor. I knew he was in trouble because of the men who'd died, and I thought I could help things along a little."

"So that's why you told Mrs. Winthrop you wanted money from her. You wanted to mess up Astor's little romance."

"That's right. I didn't think she'd pay me, but it would have been fine if she had. Either way, it was more trouble for Astor."

"You son of a bitch," Astor said. "I never did a thing to you."

Astor probably believed that, Fargo thought. But Daly didn't. He said, "You never think about what you do to other people, Astor. Or maybe you just don't care."

"What about me?" Fargo said. "What did I ever do to you?"

"Nothing at all. But you were looking out for Astor. I thought you might even get him out of some of the trouble he was in. So when I spotted you last night, I thought I'd warn you off. I didn't mean for you to fall in the river."

"And I guess you didn't mean to grab Amelia off the street tonight."

"I did that to get you in that old building. I was hoping Astor would be with you. If he had been, he's the one I'd have been after. When you showed up, I figured you needed another warning."

"It didn't work out that way, though," Fargo said.

Daly rubbed his throat. "No, it didn't."

"You don't believe him, do you?" Astor said. "He's lying. He's the one who killed those men, and when that didn't work, he tried something else."

"I don't think so," Fargo said.

Astor didn't protest. Instead, he turned to the wall and grabbed the billiard cue. He raised it over his head and prepared to bring it down on Daly in a skull-crushing blow.

Fargo took hold of Astor's arms and forced the gambler back hard against the wall. He struck it with a thud. The room shook and dust filtered down from the ceiling.

"Drop the cue," Fargo said, tightening his grip.

Astor plainly wanted to hit someone, and it didn't matter whether it was Daly or Fargo. The Trailsman squeezed harder on Astor's arms, and the gambler's face turned brick red. The cue fell clattering to the floor.

"You're out to get me, too, Fargo," Astor said.

Fargo glared into Astor's eyes. "No, I'm not. And whether you like it or not, I'm going to take care of you until the big game is over. After that, I don't care. Your sister can find somebody else to do the job, or she can let you hang."

"Fargo," Amelia said.

Fargo released Astor's arms and turned to look at her.

"What?" he said.

Amelia pointed to the bed, which was now empty. Daly was gone.

"He went out the window," Amelia said. "I didn't try to stop him."

Fargo didn't think she could have even if she'd made the effort. He said, "I don't think he'll bother us any more. He probably just wants to get out of town and get away from Astor."

"You're crazy," Astor said. "He'll just kill whoever wins big from me."

"You know how you can put a stop to that," Fargo said.

"How?"

"Don't lose."

"There never was a gambler so good he didn't lose now and then," Astor said.

"Then don't play."

"You know better than that, Fargo. As long as there's a game, I'm going to play. If you're really taking care of me, you won't let Daly kill anybody."

"I'll do my best to see that he doesn't," Fargo said.

"Good," Astor said. "I'm going to my room now. You won't have to worry about me for the rest of the night."

That sounded fine to Fargo, who was glad to see the young man leave. The more he associated with Astor, the less he liked him. It was a puzzle that a woman like Chloe, who had a good heart and a loving spirit, could be from the same family.

"Where are you spending the night?" Fargo asked Amelia.

"I have a room," she said.

"Better than this one?"

"Not much." She paused. "Not any. Maybe not as good."

"Then why don't you stay here?"

"Are you sure I won't be distracting you from your nursemaid duties?"

"You know," Fargo said, "you might be."

"And you don't care?"

"That's right," Fargo said. "I don't care."

18

The next day Fargo met Red Herman, the owner of the King Crawfish. He was a tall man with broad shoulders, a face scarred by smallpox, and thinning red hair.

"I've heard of you, Fargo," Herman said. "You're the one they call the Trailsman. You're a long way from a trail here."

"So I've noticed," Fargo said.

"Are you going to sit in on the big game, or are you just here to watch?"

"I like poker as well as the next man, but I'm not in the same class as most of the people you have here. I might sit in for a while, but I won't last long."

"It's going to be something," Herman said. He took a small thin cigar from a pocket inside his jacket and stuck it in his mouth. "You want a smoke?"

"No, thanks."

Herman lit the cigar with a lucifer and puffed smoke for a couple of seconds.

"This game is going to make a name for my place," he said after a moment. "Before long, I'll have gamblers coming here from all over the country."

"If they're not afraid of Gallatin Street," Fargo said.

Herman laughed. "Before long, Gallatin Street will be cleaned up, thanks to me. If you have people coming into your city, you want to be sure they get back home to tell their friends what a wonderful place it is. If this poker game does what I think it will, the police will be spending a lot more time on Gallatin."

Fargo wasn't so sure things would work out that way,

but before he could say anything, Cam Winthrop walked into the hotel.

"Well, well," Herman said. "There's just the kind of man I was talking about. The city will want to be sure he's well taken care of. And for that matter, so do I. Excuse me, Fargo."

Herman walked over to Winthrop who was tapping the floor impatiently with his stick. The two men talked together for a while, then Herman ushered Winthrop away, no doubt to show him the gambling rooms on the second floor. Fargo had seen them already, and while they were hardly as impressive as the casino on *The Wanderer,* they were more than adequate for their purpose. In fact, he hadn't expected them to be quite as grand as they were, not in this section of town.

Fargo watched as the two men disappeared on the stairs, and wondered if Winthrop had brought the money that Astor wanted to borrow. Probably not, since Astor hadn't mentioned it. Maybe he was going to lend the money to him after he'd looked over the gambling rooms.

Amelia came out of Fargo's room. She looked fresher than he would have thought possible, considering some of the antics they had been up to during the night in the muggy heat of the room.

"I don't remember that I ever thanked you for saving me from Daly," she said.

"Oh, you thanked me all right."

Amelia blushed. Fargo found it charming that someone so sensual in private could still be so modest when certain things were mentioned.

"I'm sorry if I caused you any trouble," she said. "I heard all the stories about David Astor, and that's why I got a job on *The Wanderer.* I thought if I met Astor, found out some things about him, I might understand why he did what he did to my brother. I thought maybe he had some good reason, but he didn't. He just doesn't care about anyone except himself, and that's all there is to it. I don't see why you think you have to take care of him."

"I made a promise," Fargo said, not really expecting her to understand.

But she surprised him. "I know what you mean. You're the kind of man who means it when he gives his word. David Astor's not worth ten minutes of your time."

Fargo didn't disagree with her. He said, "A promise is a promise."

"To you, it is. It wouldn't mean a thing to him."

Again, Fargo didn't disagree. The better he got to know Astor, the less he liked him. That seemed to be the case with most people who met Astor.

"Are you going to stay around for the big game?" Fargo asked.

"I think so. I'm hoping to see Astor lose."

"He's a pretty good card player."

"Maybe so, but it would be nice to see him taken down a little."

Fargo wondered if Amelia had already tried taking Astor down by stealing his money. She would have had time after leaving his cabin. Would anyone else have had a key? Fargo wished he'd had more time to question Daly. He could have asked him about the money, but Astor had interfered and Fargo lost his chance. He didn't think he'd be seeing Daly again any time soon.

But he did see plenty of other gamblers. As the hours passed, they all drifted into the King Crawfish.

Some of them were so well known that even Fargo had heard of them. There was Gold-Tooth Charlie, who hailed from Texas; Poker Sally, who'd played and won on every boat that floated on the Mississippi; Jack the Gent, who'd never played west of Philadelphia until now; Ante-Up Tom; Hide-Poke Slim; Plantation John.

And there were others that Fargo had never heard of because they were just journeymen players or amateurs who were hoping to get lucky in a high-stakes game. They were of all kinds: men from the West and East, from the North and South, some of them flush with success, some of them so far down on their luck that the big game was their last hope. Fargo figured that most of the latter bunch would be broke before the first day of the game was played out. Some of them would never leave Gallatin Street.

Around noon, Kenneth Shaw came through the lobby, and Fargo asked if he'd seen Daly.

"Not since last night," Shaw said. "He went out to play some billiards. He's quite good, you know."

"He got a little sidetracked," Fargo said, and he told Shaw what had been going on.

"I knew he didn't much like Astor," Shaw said when Fargo was finished. "We even talked about it once. But I didn't know just how deep his dislike ran."

"You're a lot like Daly, yourself," Fargo said. "You joke around with Astor, but you have your own reasons to hate him."

"Not me. I like Astor just fine."

"He accused you of cheating, didn't he?"

Shaw's face reddened. "I never cheat."

"That's not the way I heard it. I heard you were one of the best card crimpers in the game."

"I might be good at it, but that doesn't mean I do it in a game."

"I didn't say you did. Astor said it."

"We got that all straightened out," Shaw said, turning away. "I'll see you later, Fargo. I have things to do."

Fargo could see that Shaw was still upset when he walked away. The back of his neck was as red as his face had been.

After his conversation with Shaw, Fargo went to the second floor to see what was going on. Cam Winthrop was still there, playing cards with Astor and a couple of men Fargo didn't recognize. Fargo figured that meant Astor had gotten his five hundred dollars, and the Trailsman drifted over to the table to see how the game was going.

It was going in Astor's favor. He had a stack of money in front of him and a big smile on his face.

Cam Winthrop was talking when Fargo walked up.

"Frankly, Astor, I don't know what my wife sees in you," he said.

Fargo could have told him, but he didn't think it would be a good idea so he kept his mouth shut.

"She asked me to stake you, and I agreed," Winthrop went on. "I have trouble refusing her anything. But I can see letting you have money and then getting in a game with you was a big mistake. I don't much like losing money to a man I had to stake."

The other two men at the table seemed bored with the conversation. Fargo figured they'd heard most of it already. Winthrop was the sort who liked to repeat anything he thought was a good idea.

"Astor is quite a lucky man," said someone at Fargo's back.

The Trailsman turned to see Captain Montgomery approaching.

"And how are you doing, Fargo?" Montgomery asked.

"I'm not in the game," Fargo said, "so I'm doing just fine. Are you going to play?"

"Not today. I'm waiting for the real thing. But when that begins, I'll play a hand or two."

"Seen Ida Winthrop since you've been in town?"

Montgomery glanced at the table to see if Cam had overheard Fargo's question, but the men were concentrating on the game and not paying any attention to the bystanders.

"I'd prefer that you not mention her name," Montgomery said.

Fargo shrugged. "All right. What about Hollister's killer. Caught him yet?"

"I turned that over to the police as soon as I stepped on shore. It's their job now."

And they didn't have a chance of doing it, Fargo thought, not with the passengers scattered all over the city. Montgomery didn't seem to care, however, so Fargo decided there was no need to mention that he'd found out who sent Ida the extortion note.

Red Herman had been watching the roulette wheel, and now he came over to welcome Montgomery to the King Crawfish. Fargo left them there and went downstairs. He thought it was time for some lunch. He stopped by his room, but Amelia wasn't there. She'd told him she'd be more comfortable in her own hotel, but she hadn't said where that was. Fargo didn't mind. His room was much too small for two people.

He went to Marie's and had another bowl of the gumbo, which was even better than he remembered, and walked back to the hotel. He wasn't interested in gambling at the moment, so he sat in his room and thought about Astor and everything that had happened, trying to make some sense of it. As he sat there, he rolled Daly's billiard cue between his palms. The cue was a very efficient club, easy to wield and hard enough to do some real damage. Daly may have claimed he wasn't trying to kill Fargo, but he'd come a little too close for the Trailsman to forgive him easily.

But Fargo didn't think Daly had killed the men who'd beaten Astor at cards. Daly was willing to take a few risks, like most gamblers, but his main interest was in making sure nobody helped Astor, not in doing anything else to him.

Amelia was a puzzle. She had fooled Fargo into thinking she was a naive young woman, and Fargo didn't like that. She was smart enough to get a job on a steamboat and get close to Astor, and she had certainly been following him. In fact, she'd told Fargo that herself.

Fargo remembered that Astor had thought Amelia and Daly were working together. That might explain why she had let Daly escape so easily. She had called out, but only when it was too late. Daly had been gone.

And then there was Shaw. No matter what he said, it was plain that he was still resentful about Astor's accusation of cheating. Fargo figured that none of them would mind if something happened to Astor, and all of them would be quite happy if Astor's current troubles continued. One, or several of them, might very well be in back of those troubles. Fargo had a nagging thought that he'd seen or heard something that should have given him a better idea about exactly what was going on, but he couldn't quite bring it to the front of his mind. Well, it didn't matter. It wasn't his business to solve mysteries or to help the law bring killers to justice. All he had to do was keep Astor safe for a little while longer. He thought he could manage that, but he wasn't so sure that he could protect anyone who won a large sum of money from Astor. Anyone who did that was on his own.

19

The big game started the next day. Not too early. None of the big-time gamblers liked to get up and start the day before noon, so the game didn't begin until the middle of the afternoon. The idea behind it was simple. People would begin playing, and they had to keep playing until they went broke. The last player left would be declared the winner. There was no prize, but as Red Herman explained it, whoever was left at the end would no doubt have put together a nice pile of money. Lasting until the end wouldn't be easy for anyone, however, and Herman had made provisions for that.

"I'll provide the drinks, ladies and gentlemen," Herman announced. "I'll even provide the food. But if anyone goes to sleep or just passes out, he's a loser. We'll drag him out of here by his feet. There's no coming back if he wakes up, either. Another thing I want you to know is that I'm not taking a cut from any of the tables. I'm just here to see to it that you have a good time and win a lot of money."

And to make a name for your hotel, Fargo thought. When word got around about this big game, people would want to know all about it, and some of them, maybe even a lot of them, would want to see where it had taken place. Some of them would also want to play in a game there, just to say they had. At least that's what Red Herman must be hoping.

"The rules are simple," Herman said. "We'll play straight through until there's a winner. That means night and day. But we'll take a break every hour or so. I'll announce the breaks. Everybody plays the same game, five card draw. Jacks or better to open. One of the reasons

105

you're playing here is that you know this is going to be an honest game. I can't guarantee there'll be no cheating, but I can promise you that the punishment will be severe if anyone gets caught. Let me introduce Big James Talbot."

A man walked over from the side of the room to join Herman. He looked to Fargo to be at least six and a half feet tall, and he had hands big enough to crush a man's skull. Herman reached up a hand and put it on Talbot's shoulder.

"Big James is the one who'll deal with any cheating," Herman said. "I hate to think what might happen if he got a hold of somebody he didn't like. So I advise every one of you to play it straight all the way."

Fargo didn't really expect any cheating in the games, and Herman probably didn't, either. It wasn't that nobody knew how to cheat. Probably most of them were pretty good at it, Shaw being just one example. But the people involved were too skilled at detecting cheaters for anyone to put something over on them. However, it was good business to have someone like Talbot around, just in case.

Herman had a few other people around, too. Women who looked good in low-cut dresses were there to pass out the drinks and food. It wasn't much of a surprise that one of the women was Amelia.

She stopped by Fargo's table and said, "Can I get you anything to drink?"

"I thought you might be at one of the tables," Fargo said.

"I can't afford to play, and I don't know much about cards, so I asked Mr. Herman for a job."

"So you can keep an eye on things."

"I'm not interested in 'things.' I'm interested in David Astor."

"So am I," Fargo said.

Fargo found himself seated at a table with Hide-Poke Slim and two men he didn't know. Their names were Ferris and Norton. Slim was tall with a big nose and watery blue eyes. He was known for preferring to keep most of his poke in his pockets and out of sight of the other players. He didn't like for them to know how far behind, or ahead, he was in the game. Under ordinary circumstances, most other players didn't mind, but these weren't ordinary circumstances. Red Herman came around to remind Slim to keep his money in sight.

Ferris was nervous. He was sweating even more than the close air in the room called for, and he kept darting glances at the other players. When they made eye contact, he would look away.

Norton was just the opposite. He looked so cool that he might have been sitting in the snow on a mountain top. His gaze was steady, and his eyes were clear.

Fargo had a few rules about playing poker. Not that he'd ever thought of them as rules. They were just things he thought made a difference in any kind of game of chance. One of the rules was that he never played with a man who couldn't afford to lose. Ferris looked like that kind of player.

The problem with a desperate man at the table was that he would spoil the game for the others and make it hard for them to know what to do. A desperate man would bluff when he shouldn't, and he'd likely as not throw in a good hand without knowing it. It was best to get someone like that out of the game as soon as possible, and Fargo was sure Slim was thinking the same thing. He didn't know about Norton.

Ferris was even worse than Fargo had anticipated. He raised when he shouldn't, bet on hands that even a beginner would have folded, and generally proved to be completely inept. Between hands he would mop his head with a handkerchief that may have once been white but was now stained a light shade of yellowish brown. By the time he'd lost the first four hands, he was muttering to himself. The muttering got worse as his losses mounted.

Norton didn't seem to notice, but Slim looked across the table and gave Fargo an almost imperceptible nod. Neither of them showed Ferris any mercy, and before long the nervous man was broke and out of the game. His neck was red and swollen with anger, but before he could say or do anything that would cause a disruption, Big Jim Talbot was there. He put a heavy hand on Ferris's shoulder and turned him from the table. He had him on his way out of the room before people at the other tables even noticed what was going on.

Slim called for a drink, and they took a short break from

playing, but nobody said a word. When they got back to the game, Fargo's intent was to get Norton next. It took a while, but Norton began to lose now and then, and finally tapped out when Slim beat his three jacks with a small straight.

"I salute you, gentlemen," Norton said, standing up. "I thought I was a better player than I've shown today."

"You did fine," Slim said. "You don't show much, and you played what you were dealt."

It was as much of a compliment as anyone was likely to get from Slim, and Norton seemed to know it. He turned and left without another word.

"You and me now, Trailsman," Slim said.

Fargo nodded and tossed in his ante.

Another of Fargo's rules was that you had to have patience. Money helped, of course. It helped a lot. It was generally true in Fargo's experience that whoever started with the most money was the one who came out the big winner, but even then the man with the money needed patience to ride out the bad hands. When you didn't have a lot of money, patience was the next best thing. So Fargo decided that the only chance he had to beat Slim was to be very careful, and very patient. That meant not betting on bad hands, not doing anything stupid like drawing to a three-card flush or an inside straight, or trying a bluff on a hand that wasn't worth it.

As they played, Fargo wondered just why he was in the game in the first place. He hadn't really planned to play. After all, his job was simply to be Astor's nursemaid. But the lure of the money and the chance to match wits with some of the best poker players in the country had turned out to be too much to resist. Fargo was glad that he'd managed to put aside a little stake for himself. He couldn't really afford to lose it all, but then he wasn't planning to risk it all. Just what he'd brought into the room with him. If that was enough to keep him in the game for a while, that was fine with him.

After quite a few hands, Fargo got lucky. He was dealt three kings. Neither man had been able to get much advantage to this point, but Slim raised Fargo's bet, and Fargo figured him for a good hand, too. It was time to see how patient Slim could be when he thought he had a chance to win big.

Fargo took two cards, and drew a fourth king. This was his chance, and he took advantage of it, pulling a reverse bluff by hesitating and letting Slim think he wasn't certain that he should bet. But bet he did, and Slim raised. Fargo hesitated again, then raised. The pot was very respectable now, and Slim didn't hesitate at all. He raised big, and Fargo called.

If Slim was upset when Fargo laid his hand, he didn't show it.

"Not bad," he said, folding his own hand. "I wish I'd known you were such a good player, Fargo."

"Not so good. Just lucky."

Slim smiled a thin smile and said nothing. From that point on, his luck went downhill, and he finally threw in his last hand.

"That's all for me, Fargo. You play a mean hand of poker. If you ever want to give up the trail, you might be able to make a living at the tables."

Fargo didn't even consider the possibility. Sitting in a room full of people, smelling their cigar smoke and their whiskey, was no kind of life for him. He wanted to be out under the open sky where you could smell the clean air of the prairies and the mountains.

"I think I'll stick to the trail," he said.

Slim shrugged. "Everybody has something he likes best. Me, I like this."

He held out a hand to indicate the crowded room. Fargo saw David Astor sitting quietly at one table with Poker Sally. Captain Montgomery was at another, where there were still two other players. Amelia moved around the room with drinks on a tray. There was very little noise, and the air was thick with heat. Smoke hung along the ceiling in a thin cloud, and the smell of it mingled with the dank odor of the outside air that came in through the open windows.

"I don't think I'd last long in places like this," Fargo said.

Slim shrugged again, stood up, and put out a hand.

"It was a pleasure to try out your game," he said.

Fargo shook his hand and said, "Maybe we'll do it again one of these days."

"If we do, it won't come out the same."

Fargo nodded. He figured that Slim was right.

Slim left after they had shared a drink, and Fargo was surprised to see that it was late afternoon. He'd been so intent on the cards that he hadn't noticed how much time had passed.

But the coming on of evening didn't mean that the game was over. It was just getting started. One of the things required for a game like this was stamina. There was an occasional break, but the game was essentially nonstop. Fargo wondered who would be the first to leave because of sheer exhaustion.

He knew one thing. It wasn't going to be him.

20

Ida Winthrop came into the room a little after the sky outside had darkened. The darkness did nothing to lower the temperature in the room, and Ida did her part to raise it. As Fargo had already observed, she radiated sex the way a stove gave out heat, and every man there was intensely aware of her.

But the men were also professionals, and they knew that concentration was essential to winning. Most of them, while not able to ignore her, were at least able to assign her to a part of their minds that they weren't using to play cards. Even at that, however, she was something of a distraction.

Red Herman didn't seem to mind at all. He preened for her and made her welcome. Not many respectable women had come to watch the game, and none of those who had could match Ida for beauty.

Fargo found himself at a table with three men who may

or may not have been professional gamblers. It was impossible to tell by the way they played, and while quite a bit of money changed hands over the course of the last couple of hours, no one was ahead by any appreciable amount. Everyone was playing conservatively, everyone was patient, and nobody was winning big.

The three men all showed an interest in Ida, which Fargo figured was only natural, and they were very interested when he mentioned that he knew her.

"She's married to that man over there," Fargo said, tilting his head in the direction of Cam Winthrop, who sat two tables away. "The one with the cane."

Winthrop wasn't using his cane, of course, but it lay on the floor beside his chair. Also at his table were David Astor, Captain Montgomery, and Kenneth Shaw.

"She doesn't seem too interested in him if he's her husband," said one of the men. He was the youngest of the three, and Fargo figured he was just starting out. He wore a black hat and a gambler's black coat with a white ruffled shirt. "Looks to me like she's more interested in that other fella."

It was true that Ida didn't pay much attention to her husband. By all appearances, she was much more intent on the fortunes of Montgomery.

"He's that boat captain," said another player named Bob, who was short and stout. His voice had the sound of the eastern seaboard in it. "They say he can play cards pretty well for somebody who doesn't do it for a living."

"Hell," the third man said. His name was Samuel, and he had no kind of accent at all. "Montgomery does do it for a living, or at least he did for a while. Him and that daughter of his went up and down the river for a couple of years, and both of 'em were pretty good. I played against him on the *River Queen* once, and he took me for a clean five hundred in an hour. But he decided that being a captain was a better line of work. You get your room and board and regular pay, so I guess it does beat gambling if you don't mind a little work."

"As my old pappy would say," the youngest put in, "it looks like Captain Montgomery's got more than work on his mind right now."

It looked that way to Fargo, too. Ida was standing close

to Montgomery, and occasionally she would lean over and whisper something in his ear. When she leaned, everyone was granted a good view of her generous breasts, a sight that might distract many men from what they were doing.

Certainly Astor seemed distracted, and Fargo knew why. Astor didn't like the idea of Ida associating with Montgomery because he still wasn't sure just what kinds of promises she'd made to him to assure Astor's freedom, though he probably had a pretty good idea.

Astor was trying his best to control his emotions, and Fargo thought he was doing a pretty good job of it.

Winthrop, being her husband, didn't appreciate the attention she was getting, not just from Montgomery but from players at nearby tables.

"I wish all of you would stop ogling my wife and play cards," he said. "Ida, you move to the other side of the room so we can get on with the game."

Ida smiled, but she didn't go anywhere, and this didn't sit well with Shaw. He said, "I'd hate to suggest that Mrs. Winthrop could be involved in anything underhanded, but it doesn't look good for her to be whispering to one of the players while she has sight of our cards."

Cam Winthrop pushed back his chair and started to stand up. He had already had too much to drink, and he was unsteady on his feet.

"Now, Cameron," Ida said, "don't take offense. Mr. Shaw has a point. I suppose I could help you out, or even Captain Montgomery, if I had a mind to cheat. And Mr. Shaw isn't very well acquainted with me. For all he knows, I could be here just to help someone win unfairly."

"I know you better than that," David Astor said, "and if Mr. Shaw insults you again, I'll put a stop to it."

"I'm the one who'll put a stop to it," Winthrop said, sitting back down before his legs collapsed beneath him. "You just keep quiet, Astor."

"If they don't look out," Bob said to Fargo, "they're going to have a little fight break out over there."

"I hope not," the young gambler in the ruffled shirt said. "I don't like fights. My old pappy told me to avoid them whenever I could."

He didn't have to worry. No fight broke out because at that moment Big James appeared out of nowhere. He was so light on his feet that Fargo hadn't heard him coming, though he'd caught sight of him out of the corner of his eye.

"We don't want any trouble during the game," he said in a soft voice. "If you men want to fight, you can go outside during the next break and work it out among yourselves." He turned to Ida. "I know your husband's here at this table, ma'am, but it might be better if you waited in some other part of the room until the next break. You can talk to him then, or to anybody else that strikes your fancy."

He made the last remark in the same level tone that he'd used for the rest of his short speech, but it was still vaguely insulting. Ida Winthrop chose not to take offense, however. She said, "I understand. Thank you."

Talbot stood by the table while she walked away, the eyes of practically every man in the room on her.

"Damn, she's quite a woman," Bob said. "But I came here to play cards. Ante up, gents."

No one went outside to fight during the next break, but Fargo saw David Astor talking earnestly to Ida. She stood with her back to the wall and kept her eyes on his face. She was smiling, but Astor was not. Fargo drifted over to hear what they were saying.

"I want you to stay away from Montgomery," Astor told her as Fargo came near. "I don't care what you promised him on the boat. All that's over now. I'm free, and he doesn't have any power over me. You don't owe him a thing."

Fargo wasn't so sure that was true. He thought that Ida and Montgomery might have worked out some kind of private arrangement that would lead to Ida's parting from Cameron Winthrop.

"What are you doing here, Fargo?" Astor said. "Creeping around, listening to people's private conversations. Why don't you go back to your table, where you belong."

"I pretty much have the run of the place," Fargo said. "And I'm still keeping an eye on you, whether you like it or not."

"Well, I don't need your help. I'm doing just fine by myself. Before this game is over, I'll be a rich man."

Ida looked at Fargo over Astor's shoulder. She smiled and shook her head.

"Are you sure you're winning?" Fargo said. "I guess you must've gotten a pretty good stake from Winthrop yesterday, but how far are you ahead right now?"

"I cleaned out the first table," Astor said. "Poker Sally must've thought she'd been hit by a Kansas tornado."

"And you're still winning?"

Astor turned to look at Ida, but her face revealed nothing. He turned back to Fargo.

"Damn right, I am. I'll pluck those boys like they were hens for Sunday dinner."

Fargo wouldn't be surprised if Winthrop turned out to be easy pickings, but he didn't think that was true of Shaw. And from what he'd heard at his own table, he didn't think it was true of Montgomery either. He wondered if Astor knew about Montgomery's past.

"Of course I know," Astor said when Fargo asked. "I've played against him more than once. Why . . ." His voice trailed off. "Never mind about that. I've beat him before, and I can beat him again. Now leave us alone."

Fargo left them there and went back to his own table. Nearby, Shaw and Montgomery were talking affably. Winthrop sat silently, drinking whiskey. Fargo didn't think Cam would make it through the next few hours if he didn't cut back. He would just pass out drunk at the table. If that happened, it would be the end of his game. So far nobody had been dragged out of the room, but Fargo would have laid odds that Winthrop would be the first.

"That Astor is a dangerous character," Bob said when Fargo sat back down. "I'd stay away from him if I was you."

"That's right," the youngster said. "Seems to me I've read about him in some magazine or other. Men who lose money to him don't live long to brag about it. I don't know why he's still running loose, and I sure don't know why Red Herman let him in this game."

"Maybe he doesn't plan to lose," Fargo said.

"There never was a man who didn't lose money now and then, sometimes big money," Bob said. "In a game like this, you can lose it quick. I'm just glad I'm not at his table."

"If the two of you keep winning, you're bound to go against him."

"Maybe so. I guess if it came to that, I'd have to take my chances. But I'm not ever gonna get that far if we keep talking and don't start playing."

"The break's not over," Fargo said. "We don't have to start quite yet. I wanted to ask Samuel something."

"Ask away," Samuel said. "As long as you don't get too personal."

Fargo never got personal with men he didn't know. Where he came from, doing that was considered so impolite that it could get you killed.

"I'm not going to get personal," he said. "Not about you, anyway. You seem to know something about Montgomery, and he's the one I'm interested in."

"Well, he's an interesting fella," Samuel said. "Good poker player, too, like I said."

"What about his daughter? What was she like?"

"She was good, too. Don't know what happened to her, though. Haven't seen or heard of her in a while. I'll tell you one thing, you didn't want to ever play in a game with the two of them. I don't think they cheated, but it was the next thing to it. Why, if you didn't know better, you'd say they could read each other's minds."

"I'll tell you something I heard," Bob said. "I never knew Montgomery, or his daughter, either, but I heard she was dead. The story was that when that happened, the heart went right out of him, and that's when he took that captain's job. The owner of the line owed him, so he gave him the job."

"I heard something like that, too," Samuel said. "Montgomery was so torn up that people thought he might do away with himself. But getting that captain's job pretty much saved him."

Fargo was thinking all that over when he saw someone come into the room. It was Daly, but he wasn't dressed in his gambling clothes. In fact, he was still dressed as he'd been when he went out the window of Fargo's room.

Fargo excused himself from the table and walked over to the doorway where Daly stood looking over the room. He halfway expected Daly to run when he saw him coming. The gambler didn't look happy to see Fargo, but he didn't budge from the spot where he stood.

"I know what you think of me, Fargo," Daly said when

the Trailsman got close enough to hear. "But I can't stand that damned Astor. I'd do anything I could to hurt him, short of killing people, that is. I wouldn't sink that low."

Fargo wondered just how low Daly would sink. Considering the things he'd already done, he didn't have far to go to hit bottom.

"Maybe you should stay home with your wife more," Fargo said. "Then she might not be interested in other men."

"She was never interested in other men until Astor came along. He's the one who got her interested. I don't blame her, though. I blame him. I wish you'd go off somewhere and leave him to whoever's out to get him. Then I could rest easy."

"I'm not going anywhere, though. And seeing that nothing happens to Astor is my job, whether I like it or not. So you're the one who'd better go off somewhere."

Daly stared out over the crowd as if looking for someone.

"Amelia's here," Fargo said. "She's serving drinks. I haven't seen her for the last few minutes."

"I wasn't looking for her," Daly said. "Why would you think that?"

"No reason, I guess." Maybe the two of them weren't working together. Or maybe Daly was just trying to make Fargo think that. "Who are you looking for?"

"Nobody," Daly said. "I'm just here to see who's winning."

Fargo didn't believe it. Daly had come for a reason, and Fargo wanted to know what it was, but Daly spotted Cam Winthrop, and he tried to push past Fargo and move into the room.

"Still trying to cause trouble, aren't you?" Fargo accused.

Daly didn't say anything. He just pushed a little harder at Fargo's shoulder.

Fargo pushed back, and Daly stumbled awkwardly into the wall. He didn't make much noise, just enough to attract attention. One of the first to notice him was Astor, who was about to sit down at his table. But instead of sitting, he went after Daly.

Fargo got between them, but Astor swung in Daly's direction anyway. Daly was ready for it, and slid down the wall to his left. As soon as he had a clear space in front of him, he dashed off between the tables in the direction of Winthrop.

Cam Winthrop sensed that Daly was coming for him, though he couldn't have known why. He let Daly get almost to the table, then stuck his cane between the gambler's legs. Daly pitched forward.

It seemed only fair to Fargo. Daly attacked with a billiard cue, so now he was tripped up by a cane.

Kenneth Shaw, already at the table with Winthrop, had to decide whether to let his erstwhile friend take a fall or do something to prevent it. He shoved the table into Winthrop, who fell backward, clearing the way for Daly to land on the table top.

A gambler turned his chair to see what the commotion was about, and Winthrop landed on top of him. The man showed his surprise by shoving Winthrop to the floor. Cam struggled to his feet and hit the man over the ear with his cane.

That was all it took. When Daly heaved himself off the table, he turned to Shaw for a brief moment. Then someone landed on his back, driving him to the floor, and the room erupted into a full-scale melee.

Fargo had seen it happen before. Sudden violent action had a way of spreading in a crowd for no reason other than it relieved the tension that had been building during the day's gambling. Once the tension broke, one thing led to another, and the next thing you knew, men who had been talking calmly and quietly only seconds before were trying to beat each other into quivering pulps. Drinks spilled, tables overturned, money twisted in the air.

"You see what I mean?" Astor yelled in Fargo's ear. "The son of a bitch is trying to ruin me."

"I think he was just trying to stir up a little more trouble for you."

"Well, I'm not going to let him."

Astor strode into the seething mass, shoving men out of his way as he went looking for Daly.

Fargo sighed and waded in after him.

The gamblers, tired from the long day of poker, threw punches that didn't have much force behind them. Fargo was able to turn aside most of those that came his way without much difficulty, but one landed high on his cheek and sent him sprawling across the table where only moments before he'd been sitting. Bob and Samuel were gone, but the young gambler was still sitting in his chair, as calm as if he were all alone in the middle of a Kansas prairie.

He looked down at Fargo and said, "My old pappy told me never to mix in a fight that I didn't start. Since I never start a fight, I figure I ought not to be mixing in this one."

"Your old pappy was a smart man," Fargo said, shoving himself off the table.

Astor wasn't far away. He was crouched atop a man who was lying on the floor, hitting him in the face. Fargo knew the man had to be Daly, so he tossed a couple of men aside and grabbed Astor by the back of the coat and hauled him upright.

Astor was about to say something, but before he could get it out, one of the men Fargo had moved out of the way got up and aimed a big fist at the Trailsman. Fargo moved aside, and the fist slammed into Astor's jaw. He went slack.

Fargo let the gambler slip to the floor. He wouldn't be doing any more damage for a while.

"Thanks, friend," Fargo said to the man who had hit Astor.

"I ain't your friend," the man said, aiming a roundhouse right at Fargo's head.

Fargo stepped under it and smashed a fist into the man's belly. The man sighed and crumpled. Fargo stepped over him, looking for Daly, but Daly was gone.

On the floor where he had lain was a crumpled piece of paper. Fargo picked it up and moved back to the table where the young gambler still sat, unfazed by all the commotion.

"Got you a little billet-doux?" the man said. "That's French."

"I know it's French," Fargo said, "and I know what it means. Did your old pappy teach you that?"

"Nope. A little gal I met here in New Orleans did."

Fargo didn't want to talk about the man's conquests. He smoothed out the piece of paper and read the words printed on it: "Ask your wife about Fargo."

So that was what Daly was up to, trying to coerce Cam

Winthrop into getting rid of the Trailsman. Fargo didn't think it would have worked, but Daly wouldn't know that.

A drink tray bounced off of the table in front of Fargo with a ringing noise. Fargo looked up to see that Amelia was near. She'd just slapped a man in the side of the head with the tray and lost her grip on it.

"You should find a quiet place and sit down," Fargo said.

"Too late for that," Amelia said. "It's about over, anyway."

And it was. Big James Talbot was striding through the room, tossing men to his left and his right, kicking those he couldn't grab and who didn't get out of the way quickly enough.

Red Herman was right behind him with a shotgun. When they reached the middle of the room, Herman fired a round of buckshot into the ceiling. Little pieces of wood showered down in the sudden silence that followed, pitter-patting on the tables that remained upright.

Herman stood there a minute until he was sure that he had everyone's full attention. Then he said, "All right, ladies and gentlemen. I hope you've blown off a little steam because you're not going to ruin this game. You're going to gather up the money and get going again right now. But I want to be fair about it. Anyone who wants to quit or leave, that's fine. You can go right ahead. But it'll be your last chance."

There was a lot of muttering as chairs were straightened, tables righted, and money gathered from the floor, but nobody wanted to quit. Before long, things were pretty much in order again.

Red Herman looked over the room and said, "I don't know what happened a while ago, but it's not going to happen again. Big James wasn't around to stop things before they got started, but he won't be leaving the room again. First person to start something is going to get thrown out one of those windows over there. I hope you all understand that."

Nobody said anything, and Herman accepted the silence as an acknowledgement.

"Good," he said. "Let's play cards."

21

After only a few hands, Fargo discovered that the youngster in the ruffled shirt was a better player than he'd appeared at first. He was playing patiently and deliberately, not taking any chances, but not letting any good chances pass him by, either. He was about to put Fargo out of the game, and Bob and Samuel were hanging on by the skin of their teeth.

But then came the hand that Fargo thought would turn things around for him. The youngster never bluffed, but Fargo thought that this time he was. It was nothing he said or did, at least not overtly, because he was very careful. Maybe there was the youngster's slight hesitation in betting after Samuel opened. Maybe it was the way he seemed to be holding his cards just a little closer to that ruffled shirt of his.

Fargo didn't have much of a hand himself. He was holding a pair of queens. That would be Samuel's opener if he held the minimum, though, so Fargo bet and raised.

Bob dropped out right then, but Samuel and the youngster saw the raise.

Fargo took two cards. The youngster took only one, a sure sign of the bluff to Fargo. Samuel took three.

Fargo figured he knew what Samuel held at the beginning: just openers. But the youngster's hesitation told Fargo that he didn't have a thing.

Slowly fanning his cards, Fargo saw that he had drawn a third queen. He bet cautiously, as if unsure of himself.

Samuel raised. Maybe he'd picked up a third jack, but that wouldn't hurt Fargo.

The youngster raised, and Fargo was sure then that he

was bluffing. That was the way to win at poker, sometimes. Show your opponents that you never bluffed, saving the bluff for a time when you were trying to steal a really big pot. But it wasn't going to work this time. Fargo was going to get back ahead in the game and take as much money as he could from the other two. He raised again, leaving himself only a few dollars.

Samuel saw the raise; he was down pretty low as well.

The youngster said, "My old pappy always told me it was polite to stop when you'd taken everybody's money. No need to put them in the hole. I'll call."

Fargo had a sinking feeling. Why hadn't the bluff gone on? Why call?

Well, he could think of one reason. He showed his hand and said, "Three ladies."

"Beats me," Samuel said, tossing in his hand. "Just about cleans me out, too. I guess I'm out of the game."

"Hate to see you go," the youngster said. "But I've enjoyed the play."

He fanned his hand on the table, four tens, and Fargo knew he'd been played for a sucker. Even better than a bluff, sometimes, was a fake bluff. Not that the youngster would ever admit what he'd done.

"I'm out, too," Fargo said. "Looks to me like you'll go a long way, young fella."

"You never can tell. Sometimes a man just gets lucky."

"There's more to it than luck."

"Yeah, I guess there is, at that. But a little luck never hurt a man in this game."

Fargo stretched, thinking that he might as well move over with the spectators. Ida was still there, and while he didn't want to talk to her, she was nice to look at.

Amelia was serving drinks at Astor's table. Cam Winthrop poured his down as if he hadn't already had more than enough that day. Fargo didn't know how the man could keep going.

Astor looked sober and alert, but he didn't look happy. He was still in the game, but he had the set expression of someone who hadn't won a hand in a long time. Winthrop was downright jovial, in a way that couldn't be accounted for by all the liquor. He was probably winning, maybe even winning big.

That wasn't bad, Fargo thought. Things would be a lot easier if Astor were going to be out of the game, too. It was one thing to stay awake and alert when you were playing. When you were just watching other people play, it was hard not to let your eyes close now and then. Fargo didn't want to be closing his eyes, not with Astor still playing. Too much could happen in too short a time.

Winthrop raked in a pot, smiling broadly as he did so, and Ida walked over to the table. She put her hand on Winthrop's shoulder, and Captain Montgomery leaned over to say something to him. Shaw stood up and stretched, walking around behind Montgomery.

Winthrop was laughing at whatever Montgomery had said, or maybe he was simply happy to be winning so much. He picked up his glass and drained the rest of his drink. He swallowed and laughed again.

And then he seemed to go crazy. His arms flopped at his sides, and the drink glass went flying. His legs kicked and upset the table. He frothed at the mouth and fell from the chair, his face contorted.

Ida's eyes rolled back in her head, and she fell beside her husband.

Ida had only fainted, but Winthrop was dead by the time Fargo got to him.

This time, Big James kept things orderly. People were too stunned at what had happened to think about fighting. Even Red Herman was shaken.

Fargo didn't blame him: There was no question that what had happened to Winthrop was exactly what had happened to Hollister on *The Wanderer*. Both men had been poisoned. Fargo had seen that kind of thing before, and this time there was a faint smell of bitter almonds lingering around the dead man's mouth. Not everyone could detect the smell, but Fargo could, and he knew it meant just one thing: cyanide. A few crystals in a drink meant instant death.

It didn't take a professional gambler to figure that the odds against two men dying by the same method were very high, unless the killings were connected. And it was pretty likely that the same person had killed both men. But who?

As Fargo knelt beside Winthrop's body, he tried to remember where everyone had been in the minutes before Winthrop died. The good news was that Astor was sitting opposite the dead man and could hardly have poisoned him. Not that the field of suspects was narrowed by much.

Ida had been standing at her husband's back.

Montgomery had been leaning toward him to share a joke.

Shaw had been walking behind Winthrop's chair.

And Amelia had served Winthrop the drink.

It was the last fact that bothered Fargo the most.

Ida was stirring, and Fargo helped her stand.

"Are you all right?" he asked.

"I'm fine," she said faintly. "But what about Cameron?"

"He's dead," Fargo said. "Somebody's killed him."

"But who would do a thing like that?"

Fargo didn't tell her that he had a number of candidates in mind, including her. He said, "Somebody at his table, or near him. It had to be that way."

"I think I need to sit down. Please."

Fargo took her elbow and guided her to a nearby chair. She sat down and gave him a blank look. He would have suggested that she have a drink, but he wasn't sure that was a good idea, not with cyanide in the room.

"You sit here and rest," he said. "I'll be back."

He started in the direction of Winthrop's body and all around him he heard people murmuring about Astor.

"He was losing, big. And you know what happens to people who win from him. I don't know why Red let him in the game. He should have known better."

"Yeah. I hear that somebody won from him on the boat coming down here, and he died, too."

"Well, I know one thing for sure and certain, and that's that I'm not going to play at the table with a goddamned jinx like Astor."

"Damn right. We oughta let Red know how we feel right now. It's crazy to have somebody like that in the same room, much less have him at the same table."

Fargo knew that Astor was hearing most of the remarks, but the gambler sat rigidly in his chair, staring straight ahead as if he couldn't quite believe what had happened.

A man made his way through the crowd and knelt down by Winthrop. He put an ear to the dead man's chest, but

123

Fargo knew he wasn't going to hear a heartbeat. After a brief examination he covered Winthrop's upper body with his coat, then went to where Red Herman stood in the middle of the room with Big James at his side. The man whispered to Herman, who nodded and said something to Big James, who put two fingers in the corners of his mouth and let out a piercing whistle. Quiet descended upon the room.

"There's been a terrible accident," Herman said into the hush. "Mr. Cole here is a doctor, and he tells me that Mr. Winthrop has suffered a heart attack."

The chatter immediately started again. Fargo figured that Cole might be a doctor, all right. It stood to reason that in a room full of poker players, at least one of them might know something about medicine. But Fargo didn't think there was a single person in the room who believed the story about the heart attack.

The mumbling didn't go on for long because Big James cut loose with another high-pitched whistle.

"I know that some of you think of this as an excuse for me to stop the game," Herman said, "but I'm not going to do that. It's too bad that a man has died, but those things happen, and we all know it. It's not the first time that the excitement of winning a big hand has just been too much. Some of you might even have seen it happen before."

"I seen it one time up in Denver," a man called. Fargo wondered if he was a good friend of Herman's. "Fella keeled over right in the middle of the table before he could rake in the pot."

"Winning can be too much for a man," Herman said, "but that doesn't mean the rest of us can't keep playing. But I know some of you might be spooked. You think something like this will change your luck, and I can understand that. That's why I'm going to change the rules and give anybody who wants it a chance to leave right now. You can take your winnings, or whatever you have left, and quit the game. But the rest of you can stay. You can stay and play until the game's over and there's one winner among you all."

He stopped and looked around the room. Fargo could see indecision on a lot of the faces there. Plenty wanted to quit right then, but the element of greed was strong. If they stayed, there was a chance for a big payoff. And a chance that every gambler up and down the Mississippi would know the winner's name. The temptation to stay and play it out was a powerful thing.

But not powerful enough for everyone. Several collected their winnings, got up, and left. And every one of them managed to give Astor a mean look as they passed his table on the way out.

"Dr. Cole will see to the departed," Herman said when things had settled down. "The rest of you can get back to playing cards."

Big James picked up Winthrop's body and carried it out of the room with Dr. Cole close behind. Everyone in the room watched them go, and conversation started humming.

Fargo thought it would take a while to get things back to normal, and he was out of the game anyway. So he went to continue his conversation with Ida.

"You wanted to be shed of him," he said, sitting beside her. "Now you are. So you can drop the act."

Ida looked at him and said, "I . . . I don't know what you mean. How could you be so cruel at a time like this?"

"Have you forgotten what we talked about that night in my room?"

"If you ever thought I wanted to harm my husband, you must have imagined it. I'm sure it was nothing that I said. Why, I loved Cameron."

She was good, Fargo thought. Very good. Even he, knowing what he knew, almost believed her.

"It's a good story," he said, "and I don't blame you for sticking to it. Especially since you were standing close enough to have slipped the poison in his drink yourself."

Ida sat up straight in the chair and said, "That's a horrible thing to say. I would never do anything like that to my own husband."

Fargo might have told her what he thought about that statement, but he didn't get a chance. Dr. Cole was standing beside them.

"Mrs. Winthrop?" he said.

Ida nodded.

"I'm truly sorry for your loss," Cole said. "It's a terrible thing. Did your husband have a weak heart?"

"Yes. He did. I told him many times not to get excited, but he never listened to me. You know how men are."

Ida dug around in her purse and found a linen handkerchief. She took it out and dabbed at the corners of her eyes.

Fargo was fascinated. He'd never seen such a good performance, not even on stage. It was so good that he thought maybe Ida must halfway believe it herself.

She lowered her hands to the table, crushing the handkerchief, and Dr. Cole covered her hands with his own.

"I know this is hard on you, but arrangements must be made."

"Even on Gallatin Street?" Fargo said.

Cole looked at him as if noticing him for the first time.

"The King Crawfish is a respectable hotel," he said. "Its location is just an accident of geography."

"And Winthrop's death was caused by a bad heart."

Cole bristled. "Are you implying that I don't know my own business?"

"I'm not implying anything," Fargo told him. "I'm saying it straight out. Winthrop didn't die of any heart attack. He was poisoned. If you really know your business, you'll call the law before you sign any death certificate."

"No," Cole said. "I don't think I'll do that. It wouldn't be convenient."

"I don't care about convenience," Fargo said. "I care about that dead man."

"What he says is possible," Ida murmured.

"What?" Cole said.

"My husband could have been killed, I suppose. Everyone knows that men who win money from Mr. David Astor, as my husband was doing, die in mysterious ways. It happened to a man on the boat as we were coming here. Maybe you should call the law and have them arrest Mr. Astor."

Fargo was disgusted. Ida knew her husband had been murdered, all right, and now she was going to throw David to the wolves again, for no good reason except that she probably hoped the threat would keep Fargo quiet. Or maybe she was the one who'd killed Winthrop. That would explain a lot of things.

"Call the law, then," Fargo said. "I'll be Astor's witness. He's the only one at the table who couldn't have poisoned your husband, and I'll swear to that."

"It was a heart attack," Cole said, "and we won't be calling the law at all. Do you agree, Mrs. Winthrop?"

Ida dabbed at her eyes again and said that she did.

"And what about you?" Cole asked Fargo.

"It was murder, and I'm going to do something about it," Fargo said.

"I'm afraid that wouldn't be a good idea," Cole said, and raised a hand to motion to Big James, who started toward the table.

It was clear from his expression and the way he was flexing his hands that he wasn't planning to reason with anybody.

He was going to bounce somebody's head off the floor, and the head he was going to bounce belonged to Fargo.

22

When Big James was about four feet away, Fargo pulled his Colt and pointed it at the large man's chest.

"I wouldn't do anything hasty if I were you," Fargo said.

"He's not going to do anything," Red Herman said, emerging from behind the big man. "Why don't you come with me, Mr. Fargo, and we'll have a talk about all this."

"I don't want to talk. I want to get something done about Cam Winthrop."

"Something will be done. I can assure you of that. Now if you don't mind, put away that weapon and come with me."

Fargo looked at Big James, who gave him a crooked grin and a nod.

"All right," Fargo said, and he holstered the gun. "Let's go."

He followed Herman to a door at the back of the room,

conscious that all the gamblers were watching him. He caught sight of Astor, who gave him a short salute.

Herman opened the door and motioned Fargo through. He followed Fargo inside and closed the door behind them. The room was an office, with a desk and a couple of chairs.

"I know you think I should have called the police," Herman said, crossing the room and sitting behind the desk. "Have a seat, and I'll tell you why I didn't."

Fargo sat in a straight-backed wooden chair and stretched his long legs out in front of him.

"I know why you didn't," he said. "You don't have to tell me. You don't want any police because you don't want anything to spoil your big game. People won't come here if they hear tales about murders in your casino."

"That's about it," Herman admitted. "A little cold-hearted, maybe, but I have a business to think of. I went to a lot of trouble to promote this game, and I can't let it be spoiled by something like an unfortunate death."

"It was more than unfortunate. It was murder."

"We don't know that for sure."

"You saw Winthrop. He was poisoned, and you know it. And you know it had to be one of the people at the table who killed him."

"You could be right. I'd say that if anyone killed him, it was Astor, judging from that magazine article about him. There would be all kinds of articles in the newspapers about this if word got out, especially with Astor involved."

"He didn't do it. I was watching him, and I can guarantee he didn't. It was one of the others."

"Maybe." Herman wasn't convinced. "Anyway, you can do whatever you want to with them or to them after the game's over and we have a winner. Until then, you'll just have to hold off."

"Or you'll sic Big James on me."

Herman nodded. "Exactly. He won't poison you, but you might wish he had."

Fargo started to say that brutality had been tried on him before, but the results hadn't been what they expected. He'd just be wasting his breath, though. He wasn't going to change Herman's mind.

There was a knock on the door. Herman got up and

opened it. Big James stood there, and Fargo could hear the rumble of talk outside. The game still hadn't started again.

"What's the trouble?" Herman asked.

Big James's voice was oddly high-pitched for a man of his size. He said, "They don't want to play anymore if Astor's still in the game."

"I thought Astor was the big loser at his table," Fargo said.

"He was losing, sure," Big James said. "But he's not quite broke, and he says he's going to keep playing. Says his luck's about to change for the better."

Every gambler believed that, Fargo thought. But they weren't often right about it. Astor probably wasn't right, either, but you'd never be able to tell him that. Fargo knew him well enough to know that he had a stubborn streak. If Astor said he was going to stick in the game, he was going to stick.

"What are we gonna do?" Big James asked.

The noise in the room at his back was getting louder. The tension was building again, and Fargo thought someone should do something fast or another fight would break out. Herman wouldn't like that.

Herman thought it over for a few seconds and said, "We'll have to remove Mr. Astor."

"Hold on," Fargo said. "He has a right to finish out the string. You wouldn't want people to think anybody was getting unfair treatment, would you?"

"I don't want another fight, either. I want a nice, quiet game, and I want everybody to go home happy."

"Except for Astor."

"I'm sorry about that, but there's nothing I can do."

"I'll do it," Fargo said. He stood up. "If Big James and I can't settle that bunch down, then you'd never get the game finished anyway."

Herman didn't bother to think about it. He said, "Very well. Go to it."

"Come on, Big James," Fargo said, and they walked back out into the gaming room.

Fargo held his Colt in his hand, but he kept it down by his side. He said to Big James, "I'll do the talking. You just stand there and look like you want to tear somebody's head off."

"Easy enough," Big James said.

Fargo stopped behind Astor's chair. The young gambler sat there with a scowl on his face. When he saw Fargo, his expression didn't change.

"What are you doing here?" he asked.

"What your sister asked me to do."

"I don't see how you can help. Most of the people in this room don't want to let me go on with the game."

"What about you?" Fargo asked Shaw and Montgomery.

"Astor's my friend," Shaw said, though he looked very uncomfortable saying it, and Fargo knew he was lying through his teeth, "so naturally I'd hate to see anything happen to him if things got ugly."

"Nothing's going to happen to him."

"How do you know that?" Shaw looked afraid. Maybe he was wondering if he would be the next victim.

"I don't know it," Fargo said, "but I figure Big James and I can handle just about any eight or ten people here."

Big James stood beside Fargo, his thick arms crossed over his burly chest, the scowl on his face much fiercer than the one Astor wore.

"Maybe you can, at that," Shaw said, but he didn't look any less fearful. "Since that's the case, I have no objection to continuing the game at this table."

"What about you, Montgomery?" Fargo asked.

He didn't think the man deserved the title of captain as long as they weren't on the steamboat.

Montgomery didn't acknowledge the slight. He gave Fargo a thin smile and said, "I want to be fair about things, Fargo, but the truth is that maybe I should've kept him locked up when Mr. Hollister died. Maybe this wouldn't have happened."

"You son of a bitch," Astor said. "You couldn't keep me locked up because I didn't kill anybody. You were persuaded of that."

"I don't know what you mean," Montgomery said. "Nobody persuaded me of anything. A witness gave you an alibi."

"You son of a bitch," Astor said again.

"I don't like those remarks about my ancestry," Montgomery said. "I'd do something about them if Fargo weren't standing there with his pistol."

"We can go outside," Astor said. "And then we'll see what you can do."

The room had gone quiet. Everyone was listening to the conversation, and Fargo figured most of them hoped there would be a fight. They wanted it to be there in the room, not outside, but there wasn't going to be any fight at all if Fargo could help it.

"We're going on with the game," he said, speaking so that his voice could be heard by the entire room. "I gave you a chance to leave, but now everyone who has money is going to play until he loses it. Those are the rules, and we're going to stick to them. But if there's anybody who's afraid to play at the table with David Astor, I'm sure Mr. Herman wouldn't mind if you left right now. Just leave your money on the table and get out."

He let his words sink in while he looked around the room. He didn't see Ida or Dr. Cole. They must have left, maybe to take Winthrop to an undertaker. It wouldn't do to leave him unburied for long in the New Orleans climate.

Fargo saw Amelia standing by the back wall with several waitresses. He looked at her, but she turned her head, avoiding his gaze. He wondered why. Maybe he'd better have a little talk with her as soon as he got a chance.

No one besides Ida and the doctor had left the room. Some of the players were looking at Fargo, wondering just who he was. They knew who Big James was, however, and when he moved his arms away from his chest and clapped his big hands together, he got everyone's attention.

"Game starts now," Fargo said. "Any trouble, you answer to me and Big James."

There was some grumbling around the tables, but nobody seemed eager to cause any trouble. Fargo stood where he was for another full minute, waiting for everyone to ante up and start the deal.

"Well?" he said, looking at Montgomery.

"Well, I guess we might as well continue," Montgomery said, taking the deck and giving it a shuffle. "I'm sure Mr. Astor didn't cause anybody's death here, any more than he did aboard my boat. Let's play cards."

He set down the deck and tossed in his ante. Shaw and Astor did the same, and Montgomery shuffled the deck a couple more times, then dealt the cards.

Astor settled back in his chair, his comments about Montgomery forgotten for the time being.

"How much money do you have?" Fargo asked him.

"Enough. You don't have to worry about me. I'll be just fine."

Maybe so, maybe not, Fargo thought. He said, "I'm going to leave Big James here to watch the game and make sure nothing happens. That all right with you, Big James?"

"Fine with me. You don't have to worry. Nothing's going to happen now that people are calmed down. I won't let it."

"Good." Fargo holstered his Colt. "But if there's any trouble, I'll back you up."

Big James nodded, and Fargo said, "What happened to Dr. Cole and Mrs. Winthrop?"

"They're taking care of her husband. Dr. Cole sent for somebody to come and take the body away, and they went with it."

Very convenient for Ida, Fargo thought. She wouldn't have to answer anyone's questions about her husband's death. He wondered if she had planned it that way. He'd find her later and ask. Right now, he wanted to talk to Amelia.

"I have to talk to somebody," he told Big James. "But I'll still be in the room."

He started toward the wall where Amelia stood. She saw him coming and started to thread her way through the tables, making her way toward an exit. She went through it and disappeared. Fargo didn't want to leave Big James on guard alone, but he had no choice. He went after Amelia, who was near the bottom of the stairs when Fargo caught up with her.

"What's your hurry?" he asked, catching her by the arm.

She swung her tray, and it hit him on the side of the head, making a ringing noise that echoed in the stairway. It echoed in Fargo's head, too. It wasn't a hard blow, but it was surprising. He let go of Amelia's arm. She threw the tray down, dashed to the bottom of the stairs, and ran across the lobby.

Fargo shook his head. He still heard the ringing, but his vision cleared, and he went after Amelia. When he got outside, he saw that she had turned down Gallatin and was heading away from him, right toward the worst part of the street. It was night, and not the time for a woman to be running around alone. Amelia should have known better. She was going to get into a lot more trouble than Fargo could make for her if she didn't watch out.

It wasn't his job to take care of her, but he still didn't know why she was running. If she had something to do with Winthrop's death, he wanted to know about it.

He went after her.

23

As always, Gallatin Street was crowded with the inebriated and the down-and-out, con men and grifters, petty thieves and murderers, has-beens and never-weres, the lost and the drifting. Amelia didn't belong there, and it was easy for Fargo to keep her in sight as she fled from him.

She didn't get far. Someone stepped out of an alley in front of her. It looked like Daly, but Fargo couldn't be sure. Whoever it was dragged Amelia back into the alley, and Fargo had the feeling that the previous night was repeating itself like a bad dream. He ducked into the alley and saw that the man and Amelia were engaged in an argument near the far end. They were yelling at each other, but Fargo couldn't quite make out what they were saying until he got closer. When he did, he recognized Daly's voice.

"You've led Fargo here," he said, and slapped Amelia, who fell to the muddy ground.

Daly left her there and ran. When Fargo reached her, he knelt next to her. She was conscious, and told Fargo to go after Daly.

"I'll wait here for you," she said.

Fargo didn't think leaving her was such a good idea. There was no telling who might wander into the alley, and

Rastin wasn't around to watch out for her. Or was he? The Gypsy seemed to turn up all the time.

"Rastin?" Fargo said. "Are you here?"

There was no answer, and Amelia asked who Fargo was talking to.

"My Gypsy friend. I thought he might be here. You never know when he's going to be around."

"Well, he's not here now. And you've probably let Daly get away."

"I probably have."

Fargo took Amelia's hand and stood up, pulling her along with him.

"I think you have some explaining to do," he said. "You can start with why you ran out of the gaming room."

Amelia looked around the dark alleyway. There was no one in sight, but Fargo thought he could hear a faint noise around the corner.

"I don't want to talk here," Amelia said. "Can't we go back to the King Crawfish?"

"We can do that, but I'm going to hold on to you. I don't want you running off again."

"I'm sorry I did that. I just got scared."

"Of what?"

"I'll tell you when we get back," she said, and walked back toward the street.

Fargo caught up with her and took hold of her arm, holding it in the crook of his elbow.

"We'll look like a couple who's come down here for a good time," Fargo told her.

"Isn't that what we are?"

"Not exactly," Fargo said.

When they were in Fargo's room at the King Crawfish, Fargo closed the door. Then he closed the window.

"You don't trust me," Amelia said.

"Let's see. You ran out of the gaming room when I looked at you, hit me in the head with a tray, and then ran off to meet Daly, who got out of this very room through that window while you were watching him. And you're surprised that I don't trust you."

"I'm sorry I hit you with the tray."

"What about the rest of it?"

134

"You don't understand."

"I know I don't. That's why we're here. You're going to explain it all to me."

"I'm not sure I can."

"You're going to try then. Aren't you?"

"I suppose I have to. It's not like you think it is."

"Maybe not. That's why you're going to start talking and tell me all about you and Daly."

"There's nothing to tell, really. He was telling the truth last night, and so was I. None of that was planned. And I didn't let him escape through the window last night. He just slipped out, and there was nothing I could do about it."

"Then what about tonight? The two of you must have had something to do with Winthrop's death, or you wouldn't have run."

"I didn't have a thing to do with it. But Daly did. I think."

"And you didn't tell me about it?"

"When did I have a chance? Besides, I'm not sure that he did. I just think he did. And his friend was in it with him."

"Friend?" Fargo said. "You mean Shaw?"

"Yes, that's the one. But I shouldn't have sounded so positive. I only think I saw something."

Fargo was getting tired of her evasions. He wanted some specifics, and he told her so.

"I'm doing the best I can," Amelia told him. "It's not easy to explain in specifics because I'm not sure I really saw anything at all."

"Fine," Fargo said. "Why don't you just tell me what you think you saw, or might have seen."

It took a while to get it all out of her, but when he did, the story was fairly simple. During the general confusion of the big fight, Amelia had been standing not far from the table where Daly fell. When he stood up, he bumped into Shaw.

"And I think he handed Shaw something," she said. "I couldn't really tell, though."

Fargo wasn't sure what difference it made if one gambler passed something to another, unless it was to be used in cheating, a shiner maybe. But nobody at that table would let a shiner pass. That couldn't be it.

"What's the point?" he asked.

135

"The point is that I think Shaw put something in Mr. Winthrop's drink. I served the drinks, you know, and I was standing right there. There was a lot going on at the table, but that's what I think I saw. Shaw got up and walked around the table. Captain Montgomery was telling a joke and Shaw was laughing. That's when he leaned over and dropped something in Mr. Winthrop's whiskey."

It sounded possible to Fargo. Winthrop had drunk so much whiskey that he wouldn't have tasted anything in his drink, and Shaw had certainly looked afraid when Fargo had last talked to him. Fargo had assumed that Shaw was shaken by Winthrop's death and the possibility that he could be the next to die if he won money from Astor. Instead, he'd been afraid that Fargo would find out that he was a killer.

"I still don't know why you ran," Fargo told Amelia.

"Because I was afraid you thought I had something to do with Mr. Winthrop's death. I was the one who served him the drink, remember? I thought you'd believe I killed him. But I didn't have anything to do with it."

"You ran away just because you were scared?"

"That's all. I never thought I'd see Daly again, but there he was. He was really angry because he saw you chasing me. He thought I'd led you to him on purpose."

If Amelia was telling the truth, and Fargo believed that she was, it had been Daly and Shaw working together all the time.

"I doubt that I'll ever see Daly again," Fargo said. "But at least Shaw's still upstairs."

"Are you sure?"

Fargo realized that he wasn't. For all he knew, Shaw had left as soon as Fargo went after Amelia. But maybe Big James hadn't allowed that to happen.

"I'm going to find out," Fargo said. "Why don't you come with me. That way I can keep an eye on you."

"You don't trust me."

"You said that before, and I gave you a few reasons. They still apply."

"But I told you about Daly and Shaw. You know I didn't do anything."

"I know you said you didn't. That's not the same thing."

Amelia looked hurt, but she shrugged and said, "I'll go with you then, if that's the way you feel."

They left the room, and as Fargo was closing the door, he was hailed from the hotel entrance. It was Rastin, supporting an unconscious man. It was Daly, and though he wasn't a small man, the Gypsy had no trouble holding him upright.

Fargo crossed the lobby with Amelia beside him.

"You didn't answer me when I called," Fargo said to Rastin.

"I thought you would rather that I went after your friend."

"I'm glad you did. What's the matter with him?"

"He seems to have run into a wall." Rastin made a fist and looked at it. "Or perhaps it was the end of my arm. He will be fine when he wakes up."

"Let's put him in my room," Fargo said, and Rastin followed with Daly.

Fargo opened the door and said, "Dump him on the bed."

Rastin did as he was told, and Daly lay there limply.

"I don't want him leaving," Fargo said. "Can you stay here with him for a few minutes?"

"Yes," Rastin said. "If it is important to you."

"It's important. Amelia can stay here, too. Keep an eye on both of them."

"It will be a pleasure," Rastin said with a glance at Amelia.

"I hope so," Fargo told him.

Big James was standing in the door with his arms crossed. Fargo told him that he had business with one of the players. "But I might need a little help."

Big James nodded. "That's what I'm here for."

Fargo didn't want to interrupt the game because he didn't want to be blamed if Astor lost, which it appeared he was about to do. So the Trailsman stood aside and watched Astor draw one card to two pair, jacks over threes, and then lose to Montgomery, who had three eights. Shaw, who still looked a bit apprehensive at the sight of Fargo, had already thrown in his hand.

Astor looked around the table and said, "That does it for me. I can't ante for another hand."

Montgomery nodded as if he didn't really care, and Shaw said, "I'm sorry, David. I thought you'd do better. But you can never tell how the cards are going to fall."

"There are some other things we don't know about, too," Fargo said. "I hate to interrupt the game, but Shaw and I need to have a little talk."

Shaw's face grew pale. He said, "Captain Montgomery and I haven't finished the game. We can talk later."

Fargo shook his head. "I don't think so. We have to talk right now. Astor's out of the game, and I'm sure the captain will understand."

"Does this have something to do with Winthrop?" Montgomery asked.

"It might. That's what I want to find out."

"I'm not going anywhere," Shaw said.

His fingers were shaking as he gathered up the cards and formed them into a deck, holding it to steady his hands.

"You can come back and finish the game after you answer a few questions," Fargo said. "I'm sure Montgomery won't mind waiting for you."

"No," Shaw said. "I'm staying right here."

"What's going on, Fargo?" Astor said. "Is Shaw our murderer?"

By now everyone else in the room was watching and listening. Fargo didn't want to get into things any further under those circumstances, so he turned and nodded to Big James, who came across the room and stood beside him.

"That's what we're going to talk about," Fargo said quietly.

"You son of a bitch," Astor said, and was about to jump across the table at Shaw when Big James grabbed him by the neck. Astor struggled, but Big James held him easily. Astor's arms thrashed, and he kicked backward, but he could do nothing to loosen the big man's grip.

Fargo pulled his Colt and held it across his chest. Nobody seemed interested in challenging him or in starting any further trouble.

"You can come with me now, Shaw, or Big James will turn Astor loose on you. Which will it be?"

Shaw stood up. His knees trembled, as well as his hands.

"I'll come, but I didn't do anything." His voice was a little shaky, too.

"What about you, Astor?" Fargo asked. "You can come, too, if you can behave yourself."

Astor stopped struggling and said, "I'll be fine. Just tell this ape to let me go."

Big James gave Astor's neck a gentle squeeze.

"All right, all right," Astor said. "I was just joking. Let me go."

Big James released him. Fargo motioned with his gun to let Astor know that it was still ready.

"We'll go downstairs to my room," Fargo said. He raised his voice. "Just go on with your games. We'll be back."

"What about me?" Montgomery asked.

"You can wait," Fargo said.

He'd never liked Montgomery.

"For how long?"

"For as long as it takes," Fargo said.

24

Shaw walked down the stairs in front of Fargo, and Astor came along behind. Big James stayed in the gaming room to make sure nothing else interfered with the big game.

"If that son of a bitch killed Winthrop, he has to pay for it," Astor said. "And all those other men he's killed."

"I didn't say he'd killed anybody," Fargo said. "I said we were going to talk about it."

When they got to his room, Fargo tapped on the door, and Amelia opened it. Daly was sitting on the bed, but Rastin was out of sight, behind the door.

Astor spotted Daly. "What's he doing here?"

"He and Shaw have a little explaining to do," Fargo said. "Let's all go inside."

The room was very crowded. Rastin said, "If you do not need me any longer, Fargo, I will leave now."

Fargo nodded and said, "Thanks for your help."

"It was nothing," Rastin said.

He went out the door, closing it behind him. Daly still sat on the bed, his head in his hands, and the others stood.

"Now, then," Fargo said. "It's time we found out just what's been happening. Daly, are you all right?"

Daly lowered his hands and looked up. His eyes were red, and he didn't appear to have had much sleep lately. For that matter, Fargo thought, none of them had.

"I'm not all right," Daly said. "Somebody hit me."

"You should stop running away from me," Fargo told him. "Then maybe you wouldn't get hit so much."

Daly didn't think that was funny. He lowered his head again.

"When are you going to tell me what this is all about?" Astor asked.

Fargo gave him a short account of what Amelia had seen.

"She's lying," Shaw said. His voice was steady now. "Besides, even if she saw what she said she did, it wouldn't prove anything."

"He's right," Daly said. "And you're not the law, Fargo. I want out of this room right now."

"Let me have your gun, Fargo," Astor said. "These two bastards killed Winthrop, and they've killed all those other men, too. If you won't shoot them, I will."

"What about it?" Fargo said. "Daly? Shaw? Did you kill those other men?"

"We never killed anybody," Daly said. "We're just a couple of gamblers, not killers."

Astor walked closer to the bed, locked his hands around Daly's throat, and started to squeeze.

"I'll choke the truth out of you, you bastard," Astor said.

Daly's face turned bright red. Then it started to darken. He gagged at first, but then no sounds came out of his mouth.

"Aren't you going to stop him, Fargo?" Amelia said. "He's going to kill Daly."

"Maybe he deserves it," Fargo said.

Shaw moved in Astor's direction, but Fargo nudged him with the Colt. "Just stay where you are," Fargo said.

"You can't let him kill Daly!"

"Why not? The two of you killed Winthrop, and now you think you can lie your way out of it. I'm sure we can come up with a good lie of our own. Hell, we can just pitch your friend Daly in the alley. They find bodies there all the time on Gallatin Street."

Daly's eyes rolled up in his head. Astor kept right on choking him.

"Stop him, Fargo!" Amelia said.

Fargo shrugged. "I think it's too late for that."

"I'll tell you about Winthrop," Shaw said. "Stop him!"

"That's better," Fargo said.

He hit Astor on the side of the head with the barrel of his Colt. Astor released his hold on Daly's throat and staggered away from the bed. His knees were wobbly, and he stumbled backward to the wall, but the wall alone couldn't support him. He slid down to the floor.

"He'll be all right," Fargo said. "And so will Daly, after he gets his breath back."

Daly didn't look as if he'd be fine. He lay back on the bed, gasping for air.

"Go get him some whiskey," Fargo said. "His throat's been squeezed more lately than an old squeeze box. I'm sure it's mighty sore. Whiskey might not make it feel any better, but it'll perk him up."

"What about David?" Amelia asked.

"Don't worry about him. He's got a hard head."

Amelia didn't say any more. She left the room to get the liquor.

"Why don't you go ahead and tell me about Winthrop," Fargo said to Shaw. "Take it slow. We have plenty of time."

"I guess I might as well," Shaw said, and launched into his story.

The way Shaw told it, he and Daly hadn't killed anyone. Well, anyone except for Winthrop.

"We wanted to keep the pressure on Astor," he said. "After what he'd done to us, we thought he deserved everything that was happening to him."

Daly nodded as if he agreed with Shaw, and Fargo said, "So you decided to help things along. Is that right?"

"You could say that. We knew that with you being his nursemaid, Astor wasn't going to get into much trouble. But then somebody poisoned Hollister on the boat, and we figured that things were going to work out after all. You got Astor out of that one, though."

"And that's when you decided to get rid of me."

"We didn't try to get rid of you. Daly told me what had happened on the boat, and we thought you were dead. But we didn't plan it that way."

Amelia came back with a glass of whiskey. She sat down beside Daly on the bed and helped him sit up. He was glassy-eyed, but she finally managed to get him in a position where she could put the glass to his lips and tilt it back. He swallowed a little of the liquid and coughed. He soon nodded, and Amelia gave him another small sip. He took that one just fine. Maybe his throat was getting used to being choked.

Shaw's story sounded convincing, but Fargo didn't know how much of it to believe, and some things still bothered him.

"What about Hollister?" Fargo asked. "He died of the same poison Winthrop did."

"We didn't kill Hollister. Hell, how could we have gotten into his room? But Daly was able to get hold of some cyanide on Gallatin Street, so we thought we'd use it to make Astor look guilty again. Daly was supposed to be in the game, and it would have been easy. But you messed that up."

"Daly messed it up, not me," Fargo said, still not sure how much of the story was true. "Did the two of you steal Astor's money on the boat?"

"We didn't do that, either. I'll admit we thought about it. That was a good way to make Astor even more desperate than he was. But we didn't want to risk breaking into the cabin."

"How about it, Daly?" Fargo said, looking over at the bed. "Is he telling the truth?"

"Yes," Daly croaked. "We never stole anything."

He said it as if he were offended that Fargo would even think it possible.

"You killed a man," Fargo said. "That's a little worse than stealing."

"Winthrop wasn't much of a man," Daly said.

"He wasn't your target," Fargo said. "You'd have killed anybody who happened to be winning from Astor. Winthrop just happened to be the lucky man."

Astor was coming to. He tried to stand up, but his legs failed him.

"Is there any whiskey left in that glass?" Fargo asked.

Amelia nodded and handed it to Astor, who took the glass and gulped the whiskey without a sputter.

"Let's see if I have this right," Fargo said. "You didn't kill Hollister or anybody else, except Cam Winthrop. And you didn't take Astor's money."

"That's right," Shaw said. "What are you going to do with us, Fargo?"

"Turn you over to the local law. They can do whatever they want to."

"You believe me about Hollister and the others?"

Fargo wasn't sure he believed any part of the story. He said, "You killed Winthrop. That's enough for me."

"Not for me," Astor said from the floor. He tried again to stand up, and this time he managed it. "I think they've been after me for a long time."

"That's not true," Shaw said. "We didn't even get the idea of putting more pressure on you until that article came out. No matter what you think, we didn't kill those other men."

"Then who the hell did?" Astor said.

"I don't have any idea," Shaw said.

But Fargo would, soon enough.

25

Fargo had thought for a while that it might be Amelia who had killed the men, but she hadn't had the opportunity. Or at least Fargo didn't see how she could have. But Shaw and Daly would have been around where most of the murders had occurred. Or maybe for all of them, since they happened after poker games.

Who else would have been there? Except, of course, for Astor. Fargo wished he could remember that magazine article a little better.

"Where were the other murders?" he asked.

"All over the place," Astor said. "Why?"

"Did they happen in big cities? Little towns? On steamboats?"

"Most of the gambling's along the river," Astor said, "but Hollister was the only one killed on a boat. Why?"

"I'm trying to figure out who would have been around when the killings happened."

"Astor would," Shaw said, a little too quickly.

"So would you and Daly," Astor said. "And you *were*. Now that I think about it, you were there every time. They did it, Fargo. They killed those men."

"No, we didn't," Daly said, his voice strained because of his injured throat. "We were there, sure. But that's because we're gamblers. Where there's a poker game, there'll be gamblers. But that doesn't mean we killed anybody."

Fargo asked if any of the men had met Amelia before she appeared as a waitress on *The Wanderer*. None of them had.

"So that lets her out," Astor said. "She hasn't been around at all. Shaw and Daly. They're the ones."

"A rooster crows in the morning," Shaw said. "And then the sun comes up. Doesn't mean the rooster caused it. You're not going anywhere with this."

Shaw was right, Fargo thought. He'd had the idea that whoever killed the players who won from Astor would have to have been in the vicinity. Shaw and Daly fit the bill. Amelia didn't. So Shaw and Daly had to be the killers, if Astor hadn't committed the murders himself.

But if all that were true, why did Shaw admit to having had a hand in Winthrop's murder? Killing one man would get you hanged just as fast as killing two. So why not go ahead and admit to everything?

He had a feeling that Daly and Shaw might well be telling the truth. Who did that leave who'd been around Astor all along? Nobody. That wasn't a hell of a lot of help. Fargo tried to think. There had to be somebody.

Plenty of things were nagging at him in the back of his head, so he thought he'd give them a chance to come to the front. But first he had to do something about Daly and Shaw.

Leaving them in the room with Amelia and Astor to watch them, Fargo went back upstairs to the gaming room. Big James had everything under control. The games were going along smoothly, and everyone looked more or less satisfied, except for Montgomery, who wasn't playing.

"What the hell is going on here, Fargo? I want to get the game going again. I cleaned out Astor, and I was about to take the rest of Shaw's pot before you hauled him off."

"You won't be seeing Shaw again for a long time, if ever," Fargo said.

"Why not? He can't leave the game like that. It's against the rules."

"Not in his case," Fargo said. "I'll talk to Herman and get you into another game."

With that, he turned away and went back to the office, where he found Herman sitting at his desk.

Herman looked up when Fargo opened the door and said, "What is it now? Hurricane? Flood? Earthquake?"

Fargo grinned. "Not quite that bad. But I know who killed Winthrop. You're going to have to get the police here."

"I told you that I can't have that."

"I know what you told me, but this could be good for you. It'll show that you don't let things get out of control. Sure, there was a murder, but it didn't have anything to do with the big game. And you took care of things immediately. You'll look like a responsible, upstanding member of the community."

That wasn't exactly true, but it was close enough to sway Herman.

"You could have a point," he said. "Where's the killer?"

"Killers. They're downstairs in my room."

"Can you keep them there?"

"I don't think they're going anywhere. Astor's watching them."

"All right. I'll send someone for the police. Did Astor have anything to do with this?"

"Not exactly. It was aimed at making him look bad, but maybe you can keep that part of it out of the newspapers."

"They don't even know about the murder yet," Herman said. "I don't suppose you could just let the killers go."

"I could. But I'm not going to."

"I didn't think so." Herman thought it over. "I might be able to keep the whole thing quiet, with Mrs. Winthrop's cooperation. She seems more amenable to that sort of thing than you are."

"That's between you and her," Fargo said. "As long as you call the law."

"I'll take care of it," Herman said.

Fargo went back down to his room. Everyone was still there. Astor seemed fairly calm, but that might have been because he was talking to Amelia. He was talking in a low voice, trying to keep Shaw and Daly from hearing. He stopped when Fargo came in, but Fargo had a pretty good idea what he'd been talking about. Women were always on Astor's mind in one way or another.

It wasn't long before two policemen came and took Shaw and Daly away. Shaw was dejected and frightened. Daly was still recovering from Astor's attack. Neither man put up any resistance.

"That takes care of that," Astor said. "I think I can play cards now without having to worry about anybody getting killed."

Fargo wasn't so sure. He suggested that the three of them go out for something to eat.

"I'm tired of those sandwiches Herman is feeding us," he said. "We can go to Marie's for some gumbo."

"This time of morning?" Amelia said.

"I think it's open all night," Fargo said. "This is Gallatin Street."

Astor didn't say much. It was plain to Fargo that he'd rather be going somewhere with Amelia, but without Fargo. That wasn't going to happen, though.

Outside the air was heavy, and Fargo smelled the river. Far off he heard the sound of a steam whistle.

Gallatin Street was as lively as ever. Maybe even more lively. There was no telling what kinds of vice and crime were being plotted and carried out while most of the city slept. It was a far cry from the mountains and prairies that Fargo preferred, places where you could look up and see millions of stars, all obscured here by the thick clouds. Even traveling up and down the river like Montgomery did would be better than living in the city, Fargo thought, and then a lot of things that had been lingering in his thoughts all seemed to flow together.

"Wait a minute," he said.

"You can wait if you want to," Astor said. "But Amelia and I are going to have something to eat."

"No, you're not," Fargo told him. "This concerns you."

"What are you talking about?"

"I know who else could have been around at those other murders. You never did tell me where they happened. What about it?"

Astor named three towns, all of them on the river, all of them steamboat stops. Montgomery could easily have been in every one of them when the men were killed.

"Was *The Wanderer* in town when you played there?" Fargo asked.

"I don't know. I guess it's possible. Why?"

Fargo didn't answer. He was thinking things over. Shaw had said something about someone getting into Hollister's room. Who would have had a key? Montgomery. And if Montgomery had killed him, that would explain why his investigation of the murder had been so casual. He could have hoped to pin it on Astor, but Ida had convinced him not to. Maybe she'd promised him sex, or even marriage, if he'd get rid of her husband. He hadn't had to however; Daly and Shaw had done it for him.

But what would Montgomery have against David Astor? Why try to ruin his life?

"You started to tell me about your visit to Montgomery's cabin," Fargo said. "But you stopped. You'd better tell me now."

Astor looked away. "It was nothing."

"It was something. Let's have it."

"There was a picture of a woman in his room," Astor said.

Fargo remembered the picture. Montgomery's daughter, the one who had died.

"It reminded me of someone I knew," Astor continued.

"Who?"

Astor shuffled his feet uncomfortably. "I don't want to talk about it."

"I think you'd better."

Astor glanced at Amelia. "It's something that happened a long time ago. It doesn't have anything to do with this."

"It might," Fargo said, remembering what he'd been told about Montgomery's reaction to his daughter's death.

"Oh, all right. It looked a little like someone I had an affair with. It didn't end well."

"And what does that mean?" Amelia asked, entering the conversation for the first time. "Did you throw her over for someone else?"

"No," Astor said. "It wasn't anything like that."

"What was it like, then?" Fargo asked.

"She had a baby. Or at least she was going to have one. It didn't work out."

"What happened?" Amelia asked.

She appeared to be genuinely interested, Fargo thought. Maybe she was beginning to like Astor, which was too bad. Astor wouldn't treat her any differently from the other women he'd known, and there had been a lot of them by all accounts.

"I wasn't there, so I don't know for sure. I was told about it later. It was a difficult birth. There were complications. She didn't make it. Neither did the baby."

No wonder he hadn't been there. His usual policy was to get what he wanted and then get out.

"That's shameful," Amelia said with genuine anger.

Fargo agreed, and he was glad to see Amelia's reaction. Her interest in Astor, if there had been any, was gone.

"What was her name?" Fargo wanted to know.

"Mary. I was never sure about her last name. She told me it was Smith, but I never really believed that."

Fargo wasn't surprised that Astor didn't know the real last name. His interest in women seemed to be confined to their physical charms, and he found women willing to share those charms with him anywhere he went.

"I'd be willing to bet her last name was Montgomery," Fargo said.

"You mean the woman in the picture is the one I knew?"

"That's what I mean. And maybe Montgomery is the one who's been killing those men, because of what you did to his daughter."

"I didn't do anything. It was her fault as much as mine. Why blame me?"

Fargo wanted to punch Astor, but it wouldn't have done any good. You couldn't knock sense into someone who didn't have the capacity for compassion for other people.

"We have to get Montgomery," Fargo said. "He's still in the gaming room."

"Let's go, then," Astor said, and they turned back into the hotel.

26

Montgomery was sitting at the same table where he and Astor had played, waiting for other players to drop out so he could get in a new game. He looked up when Fargo and the others came through the door and seemed surprised to see them. Before they could cross the room to him, he got up and met them.

"What's going on?" he asked. "Where's Shaw?"

"He's gone to jail," Fargo said. "And I think you'll be going there, too."

"What for? I haven't done anything."

"I think you have. You've tried to ruin Astor's life, and to do that you've killed a few people."

Montgomery laughed. "Now why would I do a thing like that?"

"Because of what happened to your daughter," Fargo said.

Montgomery's face changed. The laughter was gone, and a hardness took its place. He looked at Astor with burning eyes, and Fargo knew he was right.

"I'm not going anywhere," Montgomery said. "Not until I've finished what I started."

Fargo drew his Colt and said, "You can forget about that."

"That's what you think," Amelia said, and Fargo felt something hard rammed into his back. "Put the pistol back in the holster, and smile while you're doing it."

Fargo figured she had some kind of derringer, which might or might not kill him if she pulled the trigger. But he didn't see any percentage in finding out for sure. He holstered the Colt and said, "So you were in it all along."

Montgomery was smiling again. "I had two daughters."

No wonder that picture in Montgomery's room had looked familiar.

"Amelia decided not long ago that she'd help me out," Montgomery continued. "And so she has. Now why don't you give a wave to your big friend James, and we'll all go downstairs."

Fargo was afraid that Astor would make an ill-considered move, but the gambler was too stunned by what he'd heard to react. It was just as well. Amelia would shoot Fargo if Astor tried anything. And she'd shoot him if he tried to signal Big James, too. Fargo did what he was told, and Big James smiled and nodded.

"That's it," Montgomery said. "Let's get out of here."

"You heard him, Fargo," Amelia said. "Move."

She was no longer the naive young woman she had been. Her voice was lower, harder, and more determined.

"We'll stop in your room, Fargo," Montgomery said when they got to the bottom of the stairs.

"You had me fooled," Fargo said to Amelia as Montgomery opened the door to the room and ushered them in. "You did let Daly get out of here. Were you working with him, too?"

"No." She jabbed Fargo with her pistol. "But he was useful to us even if he didn't know it. So I used him. Now get in the room."

Fargo went in, and Montgomery closed the door.

"You used me, too," Fargo said.

"She's an accomplished actress," Montgomery said. "She was on the stage in Philadelphia for a while, and she got good notices. Isn't that right, Amelia?"

"Yes," she said, "and I'll be going back soon. As soon as Astor is taken care of."

"We'll have to decide what to do about him," Montgomery said. He lifted Fargo's Colt from its holster and hefted it. "Maybe Fargo can kill him for us."

"Fargo!" Astor said, coming out of his stupor. "You wouldn't do that!"

"He won't have to," Montgomery said. "He's not the only one who can use a Colt. I'm talking more about appearances than reality. If you're found in here shot by a Colt that's in his hand, and he's shot by a derringer that's in your hand, everyone will know what happened."

Chloe was going to be very disappointed in him, Fargo thought. Instead of protecting Astor, he was going to be accused of killing him. And, of course, Montgomery was right. Everyone would believe that Fargo and Astor had shot each other, especially if Montgomery concocted a good story.

He apparently had one in mind. He said to his daughter, "I'm sure you could give a fine performance as a woman whose beauty drove two men to shoot it out, my dear."

"It would be a pleasure," she said.

"I'm sorry that I couldn't finish my plan," Montgomery said. "If Daly and Shaw hadn't interrupted me with their clumsy murder of Winthrop, things would have gotten much worse for you, Astor."

Astor stared at him blankly, wondering how things could possibly get worse.

Montgomery was glad to explain. He said, "I was going to keep killing people who won money from you whenever I happened to be around. Eventually it wouldn't matter what kind of alibi you had. You'd never get in another game. People would shun you wherever you went, which would be only right, considering the kind of scum you are."

Fargo understood now why Montgomery hadn't kept Astor in custody on the steamboat. It wasn't just Ida and whatever deal they'd made. It was the fact that he wanted Astor on the loose. How else could he carry out his plan? He'd used Ida like he used everyone else, all as part of his crazy scheme to ruin Astor's life.

"How'd you let yourself get involved in this mess?" Fargo asked Amelia. "You don't seem as crazy as your father."

Amelia ground the little pistol against his backbone.

"Don't talk that way about him," she said. "Mary's death nearly destroyed him, and when he asked for my help, I was glad to join him. I loved Mary as much as he did, and what Astor did to her couldn't go unpunished."

"I didn't do anything," Astor said. There was a plaintive note in his voice. "I loved her."

"You don't know the meaning of the word," Amelia said. "But that's enough talking. Go sit in the chair, Astor."

Astor walked woodenly to the chair and sat in it with his back to the wall. It was hotter and more humid in the room than it had ever been, and he was perspiring freely. Or maybe it wasn't any hotter, Fargo thought. Maybe Astor was just scared. If he was, Fargo didn't blame him.

"You can sit on the bed, Fargo," Montgomery said. "But don't try to go out the window."

"You could put it down," Amelia said.

Fargo seemed to recall that the window was closed when he was last in the room. He wondered who had opened it.

"Nobody could be in this hotbox with the window down," Montgomery said. "We'll just have to be sure Fargo doesn't go anywhere. Which he won't. Right, Fargo?"

Fargo didn't see that he had much choice, not with one gun in his back and another in the hands of Montgomery. He sat on the bed, which sagged beneath him, and thought about Amelia and how much she'd enjoyed being there with him. He wondered how much of that had been acting and how much had been real, not that it mattered much now. Whatever pleasure she'd taken in it had been forgotten.

"Shooting us will make plenty of noise," Fargo said. "How are you going to explain what you're doing in here?"

"We won't have to explain a thing," Montgomery said. "By the time anybody comes, we'll be gone. Through the window. That way nobody in the lobby will see us leave. And nobody on Gallatin Street will care."

He was right about that. Nobody on the street would think twice about a man and a woman coming out of an alley in the darkness. It happened all the time. Fargo eased back toward the window. If he could just fall out into the alley, he might get away. Astor wouldn't, but maybe they wouldn't kill him with Fargo on the loose.

"That's just about far enough for you to go," Montgomery said, aiming the Colt at Fargo. "I wouldn't want you to leave us. As it is, you might fall out the window when Amelia shoots you. That's fine, though. It might work out even better that way."

Fargo could see that it would. He'd be lying in the alley, and they could put the pistol in his hand just as easily there as in the room. He didn't think a derringer had enough kick to knock him backward, however.

"Which one dies first?" Amelia asked.

Fargo could see that she was indeed holding a derringer, one of the little over and under models that could fire two shots. It would take at least two shots from the small caliber gun to kill Fargo unless she shot him in the eye or the heart. Hitting the heart wasn't as easy as it sounded, even from close range, as Fargo knew from experience. He might have a chance to overpower her. He tensed his muscles for a try.

"Don't do it, Fargo," Montgomery said. "I'd just as soon kill you with the Colt. It might look funny, but the police won't care, not with two dead men to blame things on. And it's Gallatin Street, after all."

"You could be right," Fargo said.

"Could be? There's no question of it. Now, Amelia, why don't you put Fargo out of his misery."

Fargo thought that Astor might try some distraction, but he just sat where he was. So Fargo was going to risk even the Colt, until he felt something at his back. He didn't react, though it was hard not to. He slipped his hand behind his back, however, and his fingers closed over the haft of a knife.

"I warned you about the window," Montgomery said, thinking that Fargo was about to try an escape. "Shoot him, Amelia."

She didn't get the chance. Fargo's hand flashed out from behind his back, and the knife flew across the room and into Amelia's shoulder. She screamed and fired the derringer into the ceiling.

"Amelia!" Montgomery cried, taking his eyes off Fargo, who jumped off the bed to grab him.

But Montgomery wasn't distracted for long. He turned back and shot at the spot where Fargo had been.

Fargo heard the bullet buzz by his head and strike the drooping mattress. Before Montgomery could pull the trigger again, Fargo hit him, the Colt fired once more, and the two men hit the wall. Montgomery was stunned and dropped the pistol, giving Fargo a chance to release his grip and hit him twice, once in the jaw and once in the stomach.

That was all for Montgomery, who sagged forward. Fargo stepped out of the way and let him hit the floor.

Fargo looked over at Astor, who had fallen out of the chair. Fargo began to help him up and saw that Montgomery's last, unaimed shot had struck Astor in the temple. The hole was fairly small, but there wasn't much left of Astor's skull on the other side.

"Shit," Fargo said aloud. "Chloe's never going to forgive me for this."

"You shouldn't use words like that," Duma said, as she climbed in through the window.

It took a while to straighten things out. Red Herman was irate, but there was nothing he could do about what had happened. Fargo figured it would be impossible to keep it all out of the newspapers, though maybe he could get it toned down. Herman blamed Fargo for the fact that there might never be another big game in the King Crawfish, but Fargo didn't care. He didn't even know who'd won the most recent one. All he wanted to do was to get out of New Orleans.

Before he left town, he saw Rastin and Duma one more time.

"It is too bad that I had to set a girl to watch your room," Rastin said. "But I knew you could not be trusted to stay out of trouble."

"It's lucky for me that she had a knife," Fargo said.

Duma laughed. "This is a dangerous place. I have to take care of myself."

Fargo said he didn't doubt that she could.

"Oh, she can," Rastin said, "and very well, too. I think we are going to like our new home. We are already living a better life than the one we had."

Fargo thought that if Gallatin Street was an improvement, then the old home must have been very bad. But he didn't think Rastin and Duma would be there long. If Fargo was any judge of character, they'd soon be moving up in the world. He wished them well, and Duma gave him a hug for good luck.

"You are a good fighter," Rastin said when they parted. "It's too bad I had to let you beat me, though."

"I'm glad you did," Fargo said, going along with him. "If there's a next time, I'll let you win."

"You won't have to let me," Rastin said with confidence.

"Maybe not," Fargo said.

When Fargo finally left New Orleans, he found himself on another steamboat, heading up the river this time. He dreaded telling Chloe about her brother, but the sad truth was that the world hadn't lost one of its outstanding citizens when Astor died. Rastin and Duma were worth ten of him.

Late in the afternoon, Fargo went out on deck and stood at the rail. The air was cooler than it had been in the city, and although Fargo would have preferred to travel on his big Ovaro stallion, there were times when being on the river were quite enjoyable. The sun was going down, turning the water red as blood and setting fire to the clouds on the horizon. There was a slight breeze, and the sound of the paddle wheel was regular and soothing.

"It's very pleasant, isn't it," said a voice at his back.

Fargo turned to see Ida Winthrop.

"Yes," he said, "it is. I'm sorry about your husband."

"Don't be. He and I were ill-matched, as you very well

know. And you also know that I was trying to get free of him. I'm glad that I wasn't involved in doing it, however, if you want to know the truth."

"Sometimes you just get lucky," Fargo said.

No matter how ruthless she was, she was a damned attractive woman, he thought. Just standing there on the deck, she seemed to give off a sexual heat.

"Not always," Ida said. "For example, I'm having to travel by myself. It's very lonely without companions. Especially at certain times of the day. Or night."

Fargo thought this steamboat trip was looking better all the time.

"Would you like some company now and then?" he asked. "During the day? Or night?"

"Why, yes, I believe I would. Company can be quite . . . stimulating, don't you think?"

"I'm ready to be stimulated," Fargo said.

"Before or after we eat our dinner?"

"How about both?" Fargo asked.

Ida smiled. "That sounds just fine to me."

It sounded fine to Fargo, too. He hoped the trip was a long one.

LOOKING FORWARD!
**The following is the opening
section of the next novel in the exciting
Trailsman series from Signet:**

THE TRAILSMAN #259

Wyoming Wolf Pack

*Wyoming Territory, 1860—
Where the most dangerous predators
are the two-legged variety.*

The big man in buckskins gritted his teeth against the pain
that lanced deep into his body. He pressed his back against
the rock face of the bluff and closed his lake-blue eyes to
rest for a moment.

But only for a moment. Anything longer than that might
get him killed. Assuming that he wouldn't die from the
bullet hole already in him . . .

A sound drifted to his ears and made him stiffen. He
opened his eyes. *Hoofbeats.* Someone was riding along the
bluff above him. The bushwhacker? More than likely. The
big man's right hand was pressed against the hole in his
left side, trying to control the leaking blood. As he listened
to the rider come closer, he moved his hand, wiped the
warm, sticky blood on the leg of his trousers, and curled

his fingers around the walnut grips of the Colt holstered on his right hip. He wished he had his Henry repeating rifle, but that was gone, along with the big black-and-white stallion and everything else that Skye Fargo owned. It wasn't much—Fargo traveled light—but it was his and he felt a surge of anger at the possibility of losing it. A part of him hoped that the bushwhacker would come on down here, so that he could have it out with the backshooting son of a bitch.

The more reasonable part of Fargo's brain pushed that rash thought aside. He was hurt, stunned by the impact of the bullet that had torn through him a few minutes earlier, and weakened by blood loss. Under normal circumstances, Fargo wouldn't have hesitated to take on the bushwhacker. But now, discretion was definitely the better part of valor.

The rider moved on. Fargo listened to the hooves of the horse thudding against the top of the rocky shoulder. The sound faded. Then the rattle of pebbles came to Fargo's ears. He grimaced. The bushwhacker had found a way down from the top of the bluff. Now he would probably work his way back along the base of it, toward the spot where Fargo waited. He wouldn't be able to avoid a showdown after all.

The bushwhacker was to his left. Fargo looked to his right. Farther along that way, the rock wall jutted out. That would be a decent place for an ambush of his own, Fargo decided. Moving with a quiet grace that was unusual in such a big man, especially one who was injured, he slid along the face of the bluff and ducked around the outcropping. The wound in his side still throbbed unmercifully, but he was able to shove the pain far into the back of his mind where he could ignore it for a while longer. All he wanted was a fighting chance.

Fargo's keen eyes scanned the face of the bluff and picked out handholds and footholds. He knew he was too weak to climb all the way to the top, which was at least twenty-five feet above his head. But he could climb a little, which might give him an advantage. Holstering his gun, he pulled himself up about eight feet and then carefully turned his body so that his back was against the bluff. His heart hammered in his chest, causing the blood to pound in his head. His pulse was so loud it almost drowned out the sounds made by the approaching rider. His head started to spin. Fargo closed his eyes for a moment, squeezing them shut tightly as he waited for the sensation to pass. When it did, he opened his eyes, took a deep breath that caused a fresh twinge of pain in his side, and waited.

The bushwhacker was almost there. Fargo's muscles tensed. His hand went to his gun again and drew it. He didn't want to kill the man who had ambushed him. That wouldn't get Fargo any closer to learning *why* the bastard had shot him, and such ignorance was dangerous. When somebody wanted you dead, it was always better to know who and why. He wanted to jump the bushwhacker, knock him out, and take him prisoner so that he could answer some questions.

Fargo held his breath. The rider was close now—so close he might have heard the air rasping in Fargo's throat.

The horse's head came into view first, followed by the rest of its body. Fargo noted the dark chestnut coat and the white blaze on the animal's face without really being aware of it. His attention was focused on the rider, who was hunched forward in the saddle, wearing a bulky sheepskin coat and an old hat with a floppy brim that drooped over his face. A rifle was balanced across the saddle in front of the man. He was looking back and forth, and his head started to swing toward the bluff.

Fargo didn't wait any longer. He had gathered his remaining strength already. Now he launched himself out from the rock, flying through the air toward the bushwhacker. Holding the Colt reversed in his right hand, he struck at the man's head with the butt of the gun. It thudded against the bushwhacker's skull, the blow cushioned somewhat by the hat, and an instant later Fargo's body crashed into the man and knocked him out of the saddle. Both of them fell, landing hard on the rough ground. Fargo was on top, though, so the bushwhacker took the brunt of the impact.

It was still bad enough to make Fargo almost pass out from the pain. He rolled to the side, biting back a yell.

Despite the agony, he had the presence of mind to flip the Colt around so that he was holding the revolver in the normal fashion when he came to a stop on his belly. He lined the barrel on the sprawled body of the bushwhacker, ready to shoot if he had to.

Then Fargo's eyes widened in shock. The bushwhacker's hat had come off during the fall, releasing thick waves of pale blond hair that fell around her shoulders.

He had just tackled a woman, Fargo realized. And now she was lying there a few feet from him, out cold, a thin trail of blood trickling out of her fair hair and down her face.

Now what the hell was he going to do?

It had been late in the afternoon when Fargo was ambushed. He had been riding through the foothills on the western slope of the Laramie Mountains, heading north after spending a few days at Fort Laramie. He had no firm destination in mind, though he'd thought that he might drift up to Montana Territory. That would mean dodging the Sioux, but Fargo had done that plenty of times before and wasn't worried too much about doing it again.

In the meantime, he was enjoying the beautiful landscape as he rode along on the Ovaro. Rugged, snow-capped peaks rose to his right, while the gentle hills of a broad basin rolled away to his left, finally turning into another, smaller range of mountains that was barely visible in the distance. All sprawled under a high, magnificent blue sky dotted here and there with white clouds. It was late spring, but at these altitudes, that meant the temperature was still cool even when the sun was shining. Fargo had just taken a deep breath of the crisp, clear, invigorating air when the bullet had come out of nowhere and knocked him out of the saddle.

It had struck him from behind and a little to the left. Fargo recalled that, even as he was falling, he had thought that the slug had missed his ribs. That was lucky. It had ripped through the flesh of his side, though, taking a chunk of meat with it and letting a considerable amount of blood flow out of him. For a few seconds after he'd fallen on the ground, he'd been numb from the shock. Then the pain had come upon him, and it hurt like blazes when it did.

He hadn't had much time to worry about that. Another bullet had smacked into the ground close beside him, throwing dust and rock splinters into his face. He rolled over and surged to his feet, intending to make a lunge toward the Ovaro. The big stallion, accustomed to the sound of gunfire, hadn't bolted and was still standing only a few yards away from Fargo. A third slug had whined in front of Fargo's face, driving him back the other way. The bushwhacker had him cut off from his horse and evidently intended to keep it that way.

Unable to spot the gunman, Fargo had had no choice but to wheel around and head for the nearest cover. He had ducked behind a boulder just as a slug ricocheted off the massive chunk of rock. Fargo spotted a gully on the other side of the great rock and dropped into it, making his way along in a crouch. A few minutes later, he had reached the top of the bluff. It was too high for him to drop over the brink, but he'd been lucky enough to find a narrow chimney in the rock. He was able to slide down it and knew the bushwhacker couldn't come the same way, at least not on horseback. Then he'd waited to see what was going to happen. His hope had been that the man who'd shot him wouldn't be able to find him. In that case, once enough time had passed, Fargo would find a way back to the top and maybe locate the Ovaro, if it hadn't been caught and led off by his attacker.

Of course, things hadn't worked out that way. And now he found himself with a beautiful but unconscious young woman on his hands, and still no idea why she had tried to kill him.

If she was the one who had shot him. That was an important distinction, Fargo told himself through the fog of pain that gripped him. Maybe the woman hadn't had anything to do with the ambush. It could be that she had come along after he'd been shot and didn't know anything about it. Or perhaps she had witnessed the bushwhacking and had gone looking for Fargo in hopes of helping him. Anything was possible.

There was only one way to find out the truth, and this wasn't the place to do it. Fargo climbed to his feet and walked slowly toward the horse the young woman had been riding. The animal smelled the blood on him and shied away nervously. Fargo held out a hand and spoke to the horse in a soothing voice. The horse began to calm down slightly, and though it was still a little skittish, it allowed Fargo to come close enough to grasp the trailing reins.

Fargo continued murmuring to the animal. He patted it on the shoulder and leaned against it for a moment, fighting off another wave of dizziness and weariness that went through him. He glanced at the sky. The sun was low now, about to touch the western horizon. In less than an hour, darkness would fall. The night would be a cold one, Fargo could tell from the feel of the air. He needed to find a safe place to care for himself and the woman, where both of them could spend the night.

He led the horse back to its mistress. The young woman was still unconscious. Regret gnawed at Fargo. If he had known she was a woman, he never would have hit her so hard. He probably wouldn't have hit her with the Colt at all, settling instead for knocking her off her horse. On the other hand, the possibility still existed that she had tried to kill him, so he told himself not to start feeling too guilty just yet. He would find out what was going on here and then worry about what he should or shouldn't have done.

Another concern nibbled at the back of his brain. If the woman *wasn't* the one who had ventilated him, that would mean that the bushwhacker was still roaming around loose and probably still wanted Fargo dead. Those sure as blazes hadn't been warning shots.

He bent over and got his hands under the young woman's arms, then lifted her into a sitting position. She was dead weight and hard to handle, but he managed to get his arms around her and haul her upright. Fargo had to draw on his reserves of strength to lift her into the saddle. It didn't help that the horse tried to shy away again. Finally, though, Fargo had the woman in the saddle, her body draped forward over the horse's neck. He put his left foot in the stirrup, grabbed the saddle horn and pommel, and swung up behind her. The horse danced around, but Fargo was able to bring it under control. He heeled the animal into a walk. A pace any faster than that would be too rough.

The sun slipped behind the distant mountains in the west. Those were the Medicine Bows, Fargo reflected. He had ridden through that area several times. He had crisscrossed the West so many times in his wanderings that there weren't very many places he hadn't been. He cast his mind back to the last time he had traveled through these foothills where he found himself now. Unless his memory was playing tricks on him, there was a cave not far from here. Not an actual cave, really, but a place where two bluffs sort of slumped against each other, leaving an open space beneath the point where the overhangs met. Most important, Fargo could build a fire there without having the flames be visible for miles around. The talk around Fort Laramie had been that all the Sioux were farther north right now, but between them and the possibility that his attacker was still out there, there was no point in taking chances.

Fargo kept the horse moving at a steady walk. The young woman stirred and made a noise deep in her throat. Fargo felt a sense of relief. He had known that she was breathing, but her continued unconsciousness was worrisome. He hoped she would come out of it soon. Not until they got to the cave, though.

Ten minutes later he found it and rode under the overhangs. In the gathering dusk, the shadows were already thick. The young woman was stirring, but she hadn't fully regained her senses yet. Fargo slid from the back of the horse to the rock and sand floor of the cave. He braced himself, reached up, and caught hold of the woman, tugging her toward him. She came easily, practically falling off the horse into his arms.

Too easily, it turned out. She had been playing possum. As Fargo stumbled back a step, trying to keep his balance, the woman lifted her head and butted him in the face. At the same time, she drove her knee toward his groin. Fargo's instincts made him twist aside and take the blow on his thigh, but unsteady as he was, the impact was enough to knock him backward, off his feet. He went down, taking the woman with him. This time their positions were reversed and Fargo was on the bottom. The breath was knocked out of his lungs as he crashed to the ground.

He felt consciousness slipping away and fought to hang on to it. A small but hard fist cracked against his jaw. The jarring blow actually served to bring him back from the darkness that had been closing in around him. He caught hold of the woman's wrist as she tried to punch him again, then wrenched his head to the side as the clawing fingers of her other hand sought his eyes. Her nails drew a couple of fiery lines down his tanned cheek above his close-cropped black beard.

With a grunt of effort, Fargo rolled over, taking the woman with him. Now she was under him. He grabbed at where he thought her other wrist was and found it. His fingers closed tightly around it. He had hold of both her arms, but her legs were still free and she was determined to ram a knee between his legs. He shifted his body in an attempt to pin her down.

"You son of a bitch!" she hissed at him. "You might as well go ahead and kill me! I'd rather be dead than raped by scum like you!"

"What? Wait just a damned minute!" Fargo burst out. "You're the one fighting me!"

She spat in his face. "Damned Buckland gunman!"

Whoever she was, she was laboring under a misapprehension, Fargo thought, and that was putting it mildly. He still didn't know if she was the one who'd shot him, but she had taken him for someone else, that was for sure.

He had a knee on each of her thighs now, spreading her out and pinning her to the floor of the cave. Under the circumstances, maybe it was a logical assumption for her to think that she was about to be raped. If she would just stop squirming and fighting, Fargo could tell her that she was wrong.

"Stop it!" he said. "I'm not going to hurt you!"

"Liar! Damned liar!"

Only one thing was going to convince her. Moving quickly, Fargo let go of her and pushed himself back away from her. She scuttled the other direction. He could barely see her in the shadows, but he could hear her harsh breathing.

He drew his Colt, reversed it, and held it out toward her by the barrel. If he was wrong about her, he might have just signed his death warrant. But his gut told him that he wasn't wrong, that both of them were caught up in what had the potential to be a tragic misunderstanding.

"Here's my gun," he said to her. "If you really think I'm going to hurt you, take it and shoot me."

She lunged forward, snatched the revolver out of his hand, and fell back into a sitting position. He heard the metallic ratcheting of the Colt's action as she drew back the hammer.

But she didn't shoot, and after a moment Fargo started to breathe again. He hadn't even known that he had stopped.

"Don't you move!" the young woman warned. "I'll shoot you! If you try anything, I'll blow a hole right through you!"

"I believe you," Fargo said, making his voice sound calmer than he felt. "But I think I should tell you . . . I'm liable to fall over any minute now, when I pass out from the bullet hole you put in me earlier."

"What? I didn't . . . Somebody shot you?"

She sounded genuinely confused. "It wasn't you who bushwhacked me?" Fargo asked.

"Of course not! I just heard the shots and rode over to see what was going on. I thought somebody might be in trouble."

"Well, you were right enough about that," Fargo said dryly. He sensed that awareness was slipping away from him. He had lost too much blood, pushed himself too hard, fought too much. He had an iron constitution, and in a land that bred men strong and hardy, Skye Fargo was one of the strongest and hardiest. But even he had his limits, and he had just about reached them. He chuckled and went on, "Remember what I said . . . about passing out . . . ?"

"Yessss," the young woman said uncertainly.

"I reckon it's . . . just about that time. . . ." Fargo said.

Then he slumped to the side as a blackness darker than the shadows inside the cave overwhelmed him. His last coherent thought was that if the young woman decided to shoot him after all, at least he wouldn't know about it.

No other series has this much historical action!

THE TRAILSMAN

To order call: 1-800-788-6262

JASON MANNING

Mountain Honor   0-451-20480-8
When trouble arises between the U.S. Army and the
Cheyenne Nation, Gordon Hawkes agrees to play peace-
maker-until he realizes that his Indian friends are being
led to the slaughter...

Mountain Renegade   0-451-20583-9
As the aggression in hostile Cheyenne country escalates,
Gordon Hawkes must choose his side once and for all-and
fight for the one thing he has left...his family.

The Long Hunters   0-451-20723-8
1814: When Andrew Jackson and the U.S. army launch a
brutal campaign against the Creek Indians, Lt. Timothy
Barlow is forced to chose between his country and his
conscience.

To Order Call: 1-800-788-6262

S575